William Demby

Love Story Black

William Demby was born in Pittsburgh, Pennsylvania, on December 25, 1922, and attended college in Clarksburg, West Virginia, before enlisting in World War II and serving in Italy. He graduated from Fisk University in 1947, then moved abroad to Rome, where he spent the next two decades working as a novelist, journalist, and script translator and screenwriter for the Italian cinema. In the late 1960s, Demby joined the faculty at the College of Staten Island, dividing his time between the United States and Italy. His works include *Beetlecreek*, *The Catacombs*, *Love Story Black*, and *King Comus*. In 2006, he was the recipient of the Anisfield-Wolf Book Award for Lifetime Achievement. He died in Sag Harbor, New York, in 2013.

Books by William Demby

Beetlecreek

The Catacombs

Love Story Black

King Comus

Love Story Black

Love Story Black

A NOVEL

William Demby

Introduction by Ishmael Reed

Vintage Books
A Division of Penguin Random House LLC
New York

FIRST VINTAGE BOOKS EDITION 2026

Published by Vintage Books, a division of Penguin Random House LLC, 1745 Broadway, New York, NY 10019. Originally published by Reed and Cannon in 1978.

Library of Congress Cataloging-in-Publication Data
Names: Demby, William, author | Reed, Ishmael, [date] other
Title: Love story black : a novel / William Demby ; introduction by Ishmael Reed.
Description: First Vintage Books edition. | New York : Vintage Books, 2026.
Identifiers: LCCN 2025053800 (print) | LCCN 2025053801 (ebook)
Subjects: LCGFT: Novels | Fiction
Classification: LCC PS3507.E5346 L6 2026 (print) | LCC PS3507.E5346 (ebook)
LC record available at https://lccn.loc.gov/2025053800
LC ebook record available at https://lccn.loc.gov/2025053801

Vintage Books Trade Paperback ISBN: 979-8-217-00735-6
eBook ISBN: 979-8-217-00736-3

Book design by Steve Walker

penguinrandomhouse.com | vintagebooks.com

Printed in the United States of America
1st Printing

Introduction to the Vintage Books Edition (2026)

I met William Demby in the 1970s. Though he returned to the United States in 1968, he hadn't gotten back into the swing of things. This is clear in *Love Story Black*, a novel about a Professor Edwards who works for a magazine edited by upscale Black women of the kind one finds in Zakiya Dalila Harris's brilliant novel *The Other Black Girl*.

* * *

When one writes a novel these days, different factions, some more influential than others, line up to see how those who resemble them are portrayed. When Joyce Engelson, editor of my novel *Reckless Eyeballing*, listed the groups that might be offended by the book, I figured this meant it would achieve my intentions: to prod the lethargic. Some of us operate on Salman Rushdie's dictum: "Say the unsayable, speak the unspeakable."

Demby must have felt the same way after completing *Love Story Black*. Unlike the grim features of his novels *Beetlecreek* and *The Catacombs*, in this novel Demby brilliantly levels pretension with comic genius. Johnny Johnson in *Beetlecreek* is the adolescent Demby; Demby is the wannabe aristocrat in *The Catacombs*; the grieving widower in *King Comus*. In *Love Story Black*, however, Professor Edwards is a self-deprecating schlemiel, the butt of jokes, whether from his students or from the "wannabe Gloria Steinems" at *New Black Woman* whose New-Black-Woman style is captured by Toni Morrison in *Tar Baby*.

In *Love Story Black*, one of Edwards's students, socialist firebrand Melinda Rodriguez, whom he describes as "sexy as an ascetic nun turned call girl" calls him a "jive nigger" who spends his summers "loafing around Europe." Members of the Black Student Union hear about her insult.

> [A]s I passed the office of the Black Student Union I could hear raucous hilarious laughter which abruptly stopped as I slunk past like a flea-bitten dog with its tail between its legs.

In a later class, Baby Blue Hawkins, a basketball player and campus grass dealer, objects to the reading list: "I thought this class was about Black writers of the twentieth century, heavy cats like Malcolm X, Cleaver, Stokely, heavy cats like that—and here you are running down some jive about romantic love and the Middle Ages." The Hawkins dig depresses Edwards. "The bell rang and I realized I had lost yet another round with my Black Lit class, and the raucous laughter that exploded like the sudden electric crackling of a summer storm made me wish I had one of those enormous beach umbrellas to hide under."

He is laughed at when Gracie, his editor at *New Black Woman*, spreads the word that Mona Pariss, an eighty-four-year-old fallen entertainer, requires that Edwards lie down next to her in the nude in order to conduct his interviews. The interviews are more interesting than he or his editors had suspected: Edwards learns that Mona Pariss was discovered by a man called Doc, a Pullman porter, while performing in a Christian Gospel Fellowship Week (prefiguring Little Antioch's Gospel Summit in Demby's *King Comus*). Doc flattered her talent and set her up in a boarding house managed by a Mrs. Hendley, who in turn betrayed Doc by telling Pariss she could do a better job promoting Pariss's career than Doc could. It had been Hendley who taught her songs like "The Train Came By, But It Didn't Stop," and how to swivel her hips and roll her eyes.

Edwards suffers further humiliation when he attends a reading of "revolutionary" poetry for which Demby clearly has little regard, as did other members of the older generation such as Robert Hayden and Owen Dodson.

Gracie introduces Edwards to the revolutionaries, "but she might as well have been introducing Stepin Fetchit at a Black Panther meeting for all the fishy-eyed looks of bewilderment [he] received." Gracie had even warned him about this kind of reception, " 'Don't be surprised if they treat you like Uncle Remus out on a pass from the old folks home,' she said. 'You've lived in Europe too long, and the fact that you're an English professor—' "

A poet Demby describes as "fragile and demure as an apprentice hairdresser. . . . [She was] wearing an unfashionable long plaid skirt which had gone out of style at least seven years before" stands to read:

> "Black woman, you been oppressed so long by the snowman master, let's melt the abominable monster, by glorifying the Pimp, gifting him with gold and diamond trappings, drape him in vest-

> ments of precious silk, let our beautiful bodies buy him spears and guns, in the degradation of our long centuries of oppression, let us transmute our oppression into the glorification of Revolution and sacred Liberation—"
>
> The riot began before I realized what was happening around me. It began when a hefty Welfare Rights Mother shouted "Enough of this filth! Bring our men back home so they can pay the bills and help with the dishes!"

This clash between the "Welfare Rights Mothers" and the revolutionary poets has been orchestrated by Gracie, who sees profits in the commercialization of Black militancy and the Hollywooding of the Black Panthers and the Black Liberation Army. I knew a member of the Black Liberation Army. He was a customer at Pee Wee's, a Lower East Side bar that was a gathering place for Black actors, writers, and painters in the late sixties. Was he a wild person jumping out of his revolutionary skin? No, he could have been a clerk. We were shocked when he was arrested.

Edwards's last humiliation comes when Hortense, who is described as a "beautiful young bitch," decides to take up a rich uncle's offer to travel to Africa. Edwards accompanies her, only to fall ill from food poisoning. When Hortense laughs at his condition, rather than accepting her treatment of him, he becomes angry. Subsequently, Hortense flies to a rebel encampment while Edwards remains in the hospital. He later receives a letter announcing her marriage to a rebel leader. Meanwhile, while Hortense is seeking her Africanness, one of the African doctors who attends Edwards is using Black American slang that he picked up while studying in the United States.

* * *

The history of my publishing *Love Story Black* began in 1974, when I read some writings by Alison Mills, an actress on the rise, and I told her that I would publish her book. Steve Cannon, known for the salons he held at his famous Tribes Gallery on East Third Street near Avenue C, was among the first I contacted for financial support. With poet Joe Johnson, cousin of "Bumpy" Johnson (known as "The Godfather of Harlem") as the third investor, we formed Reed, Cannon and Johnson Communications Company, which morphed into Reed and Cannon, then I. Reed Books, and finally Ishmael Reed Publishing. Both Johnson and Cannon are deceased. It was because Demby was a regular of Steve's salons that I was able to publish *Love Story Black*. It was clear to us that Demby, on the basis of his novel *The Catacombs*, provided a link between Ellisonian modernists and the Black postmodernists of today.

With $1,500, I published *Francisco* by Alison Mills Newman, who had been a regular on the television sitcom series *Julia*, starring Diahann Carroll. Producers promised she would become the "Black Marilyn Monroe." She left Hollywood after a perverted producer exhibited himself to her. The novel *Francisco* is about how Richard Pryor betrayed her husband, the late filmmaker Francisco Newman, who had bought the option to my novel *Yellow Back Radio Broke-Down*. Pryor had promised to make a film of the novel, both to Francisco and to the late actor D'Urville Martin. Instead of making the movie, he took the novel to Michael Hertzberg, who then produced *Blazing Saddles*, which was based on *Yellow Back*, which I called a "NeoHoodoo Western." In the novel, Alison Mills Newman receives a call from the studio advising her that the writers were reading my novel. Stanley Crouch noted the rip-off in *The Village Voice,* and one of the scriptwriters, Andrew Bergman, responded with a letter denying the influence of *Yellow Back* on *Blazing Saddles*. He failed to mention that Pryor is listed as the cowriter, alongside Mel Brooks. Pryor even wanted the starring role, but he was rejected because of his drug habit. The great Richard Wright scholar, the late Michel Fabre, professor at the University of Paris, after viewing *Blazing Saddles* asked whether it was based on *Yellow Back*.

Disillusioned with Hollywood, Alison and Francisco raised five children, all of whom are achievers. The two became Christians and produced Christian films, but because of Pryor's betrayal, Francisco never had another chance to score big in Hollywood. In his autobiography, Pryor cites me and Cecil Brown for changing his comedic direction. We told him that he couldn't bring that corny Las Vegas stuff to Berkeley and that we were "the cutting edge." He was a funny guy but had a cruel side. I used to visit him at his apartment in Berkeley. He'd be watching daytime soap operas.

But Alison had the last word with the reprint of her novel. We were lucky to get endorsements for *Francisco* from Toni Morrison and William Demby. Deemed a "masterpiece," the novel was reprinted in 2023 by New Directions to glowing reviews in *The New Yorker*, *The New York Times*, and two full pages in *The Washington Post*, the front page and an interior page.

After successfully publishing *Francisco*, I worked on the publication of *Love Story Black* for months at the West Coast Print Center, where the printers were as devoted to the arts as the writers were. The book cover was designed by the great Lezley Saar, in the early part of her career, who came up to Berkeley from Los

Angeles for consultations. I had published her book of drawings, *Yolanda and the Strange Objects*.

When we published *Love Story Black*, Demby's book party was held at the Lower Manhattan Ocean Club owned by Mickey Ruskin, who later died of an overdose. Ruskin also owned Max's Kansas City, where my wife, Carla, and I would sit and talk to Andy Warhol and poet Gerard Malanga.

The Black and white avant-garde were in attendance at the Demby book party, including the late historian James G. Spady and the late actor Walter Cotton, who costarred with Vertamae Grosvenor in a meta soap opera, *Personal Problems*, a film directed by Bill Gunn that was produced by Walter Cotton, Steve, and me, and which has now been remastered from a box of videotapes that were stored in my attic for three decades.

Novelist Richard Price, whom we championed, also attended Demby's fabulous party. This was before he sold his soul to the devil by writing for *The Wire*.

When it came time for Demby to speak, he praised only Steve Cannon, when I was the one who had published the book on the West Coast. I was stunned and hurt. Only one of our titles was ever produced on the East Coast. That was *Jambalaya*, a collection of poetry that included the works of Lorenzo Thomas, Thulani Davis, and Ibn Mukhtarr Mustapha, which writer Kalamu ya Salaam has hailed as a Black Arts classic.

In an interview with *Amerikastudien/American Studies*, Demby writes:

> *Love Story Black* is the story of a young man who works for a magazine. The editor is a nice woman who is trying to be a hard-boiled editor. That was the world of female fashion magazines,

> the feminist reply to the male-oriented sports page. It was a competitive business. Women editors would usually hire weaker men, insecure but learned, and probably halfway famous, and not a Muhammad Ali in the literary field, because that would bestow on him some kind of magic powers, strength. I have known a lot of women who run these magazines, and they are "tough guys"! The inspiration for Hortense came to me because at the time I was dating a South African revolutionary, Barbara Masekela, who was the most important aide to Mandela. And when she left to go back to the revolution, we said our goodbye, just like in the novel. She was connected to the revolutionaries; there were many women that were connected to the revolutionaries in New York at the time. So this was a true thing.

To get her side of the story, I interviewed Barbara Masekela, author of the autobiography, *Poli Poli*, and former South African ambassador to the United States from 2003 to 2007. She began the interview by complaining about white publishers.

BARBARA MASEKELA: We have white publishers. They don't expect Black people to write good books. You're supposed to write a book whining and crying.

ISHMAEL REED: How do you rate Demby as a writer?

BM: Deserves recognition. He's a good writer.

IR: Did he ever tell you anything about *Essence Magazine*, which is satirized in *Love Story Black*?

BM: All I remember is that Toni Cade Bambara hated the book. They thought it was against women.

IR: Did he think of himself as royalty?

BM: No, I think that he was very pretentious. He was a middle-class Black person, very bourgeois. I think that he wanted to be respectable. When I met him, he had just come from rehab. It was very difficult for him. And he liked to watch me drinking, and he would encourage me to drink because he took a kind of vicarious pleasure in watching people drink. I think he was employed by an advertising company, and he had left Italy because he was separating from his wife. He was no longer getting requests to write screenplays, which was what he did mostly in Italy.

IR: What year was this?

BM: I met him about 1973, and he was living on Amsterdam [Avenue] between 94th and 95th Streets on the 18th floor. He was teaching then. I met him through Quincy [Troupe], of course. He was teaching at Staten Island Community College. What happened is that he was getting drunk, and they gave him an ultimatum that he either stop drinking or leave, and that they would pay for him to go to rehab.

IR: Well, he was drinking a lot.

BM: I mean, the stories he told me about his drinking, he was totally out of control. And I think that's why his wife left him. He could not work, but I think it had to do with his life in Italy.

It's difficult to be the only Black person in a white society. And he was, I think, the official Negro in Rome. He loved being there. And he loved talking about Fellini and all the other filmmakers. And he loved being in that life. Coming back to the United States, nobody knew who he was, or what he had done in Italy, or the book that he had written. He was very European because you must remember, he had gone to Europe during the Second World War and he had gotten his education because of the programs that were set up for war veterans. That's how he was able to start writing. And she [Demby's wife, Lucia Drudi Demby] was a very good writer too.

She wrote screenplays. He loved Italian culture. Bill was a snob. Quincy has always been very wonderful at collecting people. So he discovered Bill.

Bill watched all of you because it was an unfamiliar world to him. After all, he came from a very middle-class Black family. His brother was a medical doctor who lived in Los Angeles. His sister was also a big snob. I remember we used to go to Washington [D.C.] to see his parents, who were still alive, and then they came to live with his sister Dorothy in Central Park West.

We used to go there every Sunday for lunch. I just hated it. I think that's one of the reasons why I left him. All these people acted like they were children in the presence of their parents. The lunch and meals were very formal, and Bill was dying to have a drink. The old people were dribbling, they were very, very old, but they were very much in love. I think Mona Pariss in *Love Story Black* is based on his mother.*

He loved his parents. His mother was just a loyal, light-skinned wife, and the father was very dark. And [Bill] often talked about the fact that they came from West Africa, because, apparently, in West Africa, the name Debo was very common. If I look back on

---

*Demby's parents were Gertrude L. Demby and William E. Demby; their children besides William were Juanita D. Jackson, Dorothy Demby, Betty Payne, Dr. Frank M. Demby, Gloria B. Maddox, and Malvina V. Hill.

it, if I have to be honest, I think he regarded me as some sort of person that he was mentoring or something, because he would go shopping with me and choose clothes for me. He wanted me to dress in a certain way. He always had me wear those dark clothes, like black clothes. I guess, in Europe, that's what people wear. I like to wear bright colors. He thought that was really not done. So he's really a European. But he really adored me, and we had a very, very happy life together. He had stopped drinking when I met him. He never drank in my presence. I probably actually helped him to stay off drinking. Not because we always had liquor in the house. He preferred scotch. He liked to smell it. He loved the smell of wine and all of those things. But he never even tried to taste it.

He thought that America was a little backward. So I don't think he was surprised by the reception to *Love Story Black*, but I think he was very flattered by meeting younger writers, Black writers like Quincy. I think he thought he was the greatest American writer. I loved his other book, *The Catacombs*. He thought that was his masterpiece. But I think by being cut off from Europe he really couldn't write, because all the time I lived with him, which was six years, he couldn't write. He wrote *Love Story Black* just as I was leaving him.

* * *

Because of literary politics, Demby didn't receive the accolades he deserved during his lifetime. Ultimately, he was a man without a country, a man without a race, without a New York publisher except for E. P. Dutton, to which we sold *Love Story Black* because Joyce Engleson became an editor there after leaving St. Martin's.

No matter his mingling with an international set, he was alone. Like Bill Trapp in *Beetlecreek*, he was a literary, cultural, and political hermit, a frequent type found in the gothic novel.

Was Demby merely a privileged, pampered hedonist? There was some of that, but he found the time to work his butt off. His *From a Japanese Notebook* took a lot of energy, sweat, and agony.

Was Demby a gothic novelist who dwelled upon subjects—suicide, decay, vampirism, necrophilia—that turn off readers whose favorite novels are those that go down like a "hot fudge sundae," as one popular Black writer describes how she serves her reader base? Was he a conservative who picked on easy targets? If we eliminated all the authors whose ideas that some would find repellent, how much of literature would remain? After all, Demby's hero Walt Whitman justified the invasion of Mexico as a case of superiors overwhelming inferior people, Mark Twain had a problem with Arabs, Jane Austen with Romani people, Saul Bellow with Blacks, and Philip Roth with women.

Does the fact that Vintage Books has resurrected this great controversial novelist mean that writers can get back to goring sacred cows? I hope so.

Demby was unable to find a publisher for *King Comus* during his lifetime. When Melanie Masterson asked me to publish *King Comus*, such is my admiration for Demby, I agreed without reading a single sentence. It was through her hard editorial work and that of Carla Blank that the Demby Renaissance is underway. Finally!

ISHMAEL REED
Oakland, California, November 2025

Ishmael Reed is a poet, novelist, publisher, playwright, musician, composer, and songwriter. A MacArthur Fellow and a global writer, he has received honors in the United States, Europe, and Japan. Two of his novels, *Flight to Canada*, for which he coined the term "neo-slave narrative," and *Mumbo Jumbo*, have celebrated their fiftieth anniversaries with new editions. His novel *Japanese by Spring* was adopted as a National Project in China. Two books he published, *21 New Nigerian Poets* and *16 Short Stories by Nigerian Women*, were purchased by the Egyptian Center for Translation and translated into Arabic. For his theater work, Reed has received the Otto Award and the AUDELCO Award. Reed is the leader of two jazz albums, *For All We Know* and *The Hands of Grace*. His latest album is *Blues Lyrics by Ishmael Reed*, accompanied by the West Coast Blues Caravan of All Stars. He was the recipient of the Blues Songwriter of the Year award from the West Coast Blues Hall of Fame. His songs have been performed by artists such as Cassandra Wilson, Taj Mahal, Gregory Porter, and Macy Gray, among others.

Love Story Black

(Is there a lesson to all this? I do not know. Just as I do not know what love is nor understand the mystery of its undeniable existence. Nor can I answer the question I have so often provocatively placed before my students: "Is there such a thing as 'love at first sight?'")

1

"Miss Pariss? Miss *Mona* Pariss?"

"Who are you? You my new welfare worker?"

"No, mam—I'm—well, I'm a writer . . ."

Hastily I backed away from the triple-chained crack in the door through which her darting suspicious eyes were studying me, and I assumed the smiling expression of a kindly undertaker to convince her, and myself as well, that I was neither a criminal nor a policeman—though my nose was vibrating convulsively from the exotic stench of collard greens, pork fat cooking, and powerful incense leaking out onto the darkly sinister landing of the fourth floor walk-up apartment where the great lady lived.

"How come those people down at welfare always changing my worker?" she whined, she too shuffling back cautiously from her side of the door, so that I caught a fluttering glimpse of what looked like a tattered oriental robe of embroidered dragons and poisonous flowers draped over a slender body like an oversized flag around a corpse.

"I'm not a welfare worker, Miss Pariss," I repeated loudly, thinking perhaps she was deaf. "I'm a writer—"

"Oh, you one of them welfare *auditors*. Well, I ain't got nothing to hide from the government. But where's my Miss Hollygreen—that nice red-headed white girl got me my telephone put in. I ain't seen hide nor hair of her since way before Christmas, and my arthritis been accumulating something terrible . . ."

"Miss Pariss," I said wearily, "I've been sent by *New Black Woman Magazine* to interview you, or at least seek your permission for such an interview—"

Nervously I fumbled in my jacket pocket for the letter Gracie had had her secretary prepare for me, neatly typed and very officious looking on heavy bond paper, and bearing the self-consciously elegant *New Black Woman* letterhead. I pushed the crisp letter through the crack of the door, but Miss Pariss only took another step backward.

"I already been interviewed by the welfare people," she said, sidestepping the letter, "three times—twice at the Center, and they didn't even pay my busfare, and once by some pimply-assed dude who came snooping around the apartment looking for rats and cockroaches pretending he was an exterminator, when I could tell right away he was an inspector from the Department of Social Services by that skinny black tie he was wearing and those cheap two-toned Thom McAn shoes, and he had on one of those skinny-brimmed Jewish black hats—"

"Please, Miss Pariss—!"

"Now come to think of it—how come you know my real name before I was married? How come you know my stage name? You a detective from the Bureau of Investigation? If you are, I don't know nothing about the nigger they found cut up into stewing beef in the apartment across the hall. My motto is 'See no evil, hear no evil, and talk no evil . . .' I'm a religious woman, and I stay out of trouble like trouble stinks and trouble stays away from me like I stink—if you'll pardon the metaphor, that's show business talk you know—"

"If you'll just read this letter, Miss Pariss, it will explain everything . . ."

Bony fingers heavily burdened with many gaudy rings and with long purple-painted nails snatched the letter from my hand.

"I got to get my reading glasses," she said, "so you stand right there and cool your heels while I go and verify your credentials . . ."

Abruptly and definitively the door slammed shut, and there was the grating sound of locks being turned, and I was left standing there on the dark landing, feeling humiliated and impotent, my initial elation over the assignment having abandoned me already, as though the stench of collard greens, pork fat and incense had the effect on my already shaken psyche of a depressant gas.

I lit a cigarette and glanced at my watch, thinking that if I could get this over within half an hour or so I would still be in time for my first class of the Fall semester. But when almost fifteen minutes passed and there was still no sound from within Miss Pariss' apartment, I knocked urgently on the door—the way detectives knock on doors in the movies.

Still no sound from within. But now in the abrupt silence I heard faltering footsteps climbing the creaky wooden steps that had evidently replaced the concrete steps long since disintegrated; for Miss Pariss lived in an ancient town house that had undergone countless transformations in its century-old existence.

In a few minutes, a light-skinned Black man with the puffy

jowls and slow shuffling one-sided walk of a waiter still carrying an invisible tray appeared on the landing. He was wearing a jaunty red, black and green wool ski cap and a frayed black minister's coat which was several sizes too small for his flabby cucumber-shaped frame. Under his arm he carried a hand-carved cane with a crudely wrought Coptic cross on the head, and with his free hand he was hugging a gallon jug of red Gallo wine which he delicately placed on the sagging floor in front of the apartment adjoining Miss Pariss' and began to fumble clumsily in his bulging coat pocket for his keys. Apparently he was in a drunken stupor, but after several unsuccessful attempts at fitting the key into the lock his eyes narrowly focused on me and he turned, his blood-streaked eyes narrowed with suspicion.

"You the new welfare worker?" he asked in a squeaky belligerent tone of voice.

"No, I'm not—I'm waiting for Miss Pariss . . ."

"Miss Pariss? Maybe you mean Madam Sheba Smith—anyway she ain't home. She gone for the week. Her sister down home in Cedric, North Carolina, died—besides she already been inspected by the exterminator—"

"But I just spoke with her—I'm waiting for her to open the door—"

"You must a been speaking to a ghost then, cause she ain't back from the funeral. I thought you was the new welfare worker, cause that hinckety white girl ain't been back since the week before Christmas and she promised me an emergency clothing allowance on account of the fire last Thanksgiving when they turned off my electricity and I had to use candles . . ."

Wheezing as though he had a console of tiny whistles imbedded in his chest, he promptly forgot me and, having finally found his keys, he began unlocking each of three locks with the solemn concentration and dignity of the night watchman of a bank.

When the door closed behind him, I lit another cigarette, and resolved that if Miss Pariss didn't open the door within a few minutes I was going to leave and renounce the whole project of interviewing her, no matter what Gracie would say about novelists lacking "journalistic initiative," the exact phrase she had used when I first approached her about doing a "literary" piece for her new magazine.

"We're not printing any of that washed-out white literary chi-chi bullshit," was her scathing retort. "We're trying to get to the nitty-gritty shit about the Black experience!"

Gracie didn't like my novels and said I'd lived in Europe too long.

"You've got to take that brain of yours out of that white plastic bag!" she said.

And maybe she was right. At any rate, here I was standing like a fool in a toxic cloud of collard greens, cooking fat and incense waiting for Miss Pariss to open the door. And just as I was about to knock one last time, the door opened wide and Miss Pariss appeared, a sly smile on her nut-brown face.

She looked much younger than I expected. Gracie said their research indicated she must have been at least eighty-four years old. But in that dismal light she appeared to be a well-preserved sixty, her true age, whatever it was, betrayed mostly by the shrunken and wrinkled skin on her long claw-like hands, in both of which she still clutched the letter of introduction as though it were an official proclamation to be read before an audience.

"What kind of magazine this *New Black Woman*?" she demanded. "I ain't never heard of no magazine like this—"

"Well—it's kind of like a fashion magazine—" I lied, imagining all too well Gracie's obscene reaction had she heard me.

"Kind of like a Black version of *Vogue* magazine—"

Miss Pariss looked down at the letter again, her lips moving as she read, and then began to study me for such a long time that I coughed and involuntarily scratched my head.

"It's a rather new magazine of its kind," I said in a sinking voice. "As its title suggests it attempts to reflect the new awakening of the Black woman. I might add that it is doing quite well financially. Actually, I should have brought along a copy to show you—"

"You one goodlooking dude, even with that Jew-boy nose—you ain't one of them dancing queens downstairs keep everybody awake playing that symphonette music on their hi-fi, is you?"

"I'm a writer, a novelist—and I teach college—"

"Well you talk educated white. Those dancers, they's homosexuals, if you get what I mean—funny fannies I call them, not that I hold that against them, but I like my Black dudes doing their stud business through the front door like the Good Lord ordained—"

"About the interview, Miss Pariss? I'm afraid I'm running short of time; I've got a class to teach and this is the first day of the semester. I hope you don't misunderstand my rushing you like this. But what about the interview?"

"You sure you ain't no welfare inspector?"

"No, mam—nor a detective either—perhaps it would be more convenient if I phone you for the interview—"

"My phone been turned off for two months—"

"But you *do* agree to the interview?"

"I ain't agreed to nothing—"

She was studying me now with such intensity, her mouth slack in a sly mocking smile, that I could feel my hands perspiring and I began to rub them nervously along the sides of my trousers.

"You sure one goodlooking dude," she said suddenly, "and you say you ain't one of them funny fannies from downstairs—"

She took one more look at the letter, read it through word for word, then meticulously folded it and placed both the letter and the envelope in her sunken bosom.

"Well, I'll tell you what I'll do—" she said, lowering her voice to a conspiratory whisper. "You come back this evening, just before *The Bill Cosby Show* go on the air. There ain't no lock on the door downstairs, but when you come up here to *my* door, you knock three times just like this—"

And she rapped on the door three times in a rapid signal-like manner.

"That way I'll know it's you and not that wino bum Reverend Grooms lives next door—because he's not supposed to know I'm back yet—"

2

Promptly at five minutes before ten, the hour *The Bill Cosby Show* went on the air, I was back on the dark landing in front of the door to Miss Pariss' apartment. But now the jubilant hubbub of TV sets and the thumping basso profundo beat of hi-fis reverberating all up and down the dismal stairwell of the prison-like interior of the derelict West Side building created a less sinister impression and, indeed, I felt the almost childish euphoria of embarking on some mystery magic tour. Also contributing to my high spirits was the fact that the first day of the semester had gone rather well—and my usual air of self-conscious timidity was replaced by a deep-voiced stance of authority, enhanced no doubt by a snappy teaching outfit I had purchased two days before with Gracie's assistance (she had always complained that my pseudo Ivy League clothes made me look like an equal opportunity insurance company trainee) consisting of a brown velvet combat jacket, bell-bottom velvet trousers, and a very expensive stamped nylon body shirt with a bright red and green tribal motif.

After holding forth somewhat pompously on the importance of honesty in writing, I had had the class write a short paper about themselves in the third person—as though they were describing someone else, with the emphasis on honesty rather than style. Most of my students are working class Irish and Italians from Staten Island and the Bay Ridge sections of Brooklyn, and for most of them, having a more or less young and hip Black professor is something of a novelty, which of course enhances my authority and permits me to get away with certain theatrics and pomposities I would be ashamed to indulge in had I been teaching in an Ivy League college. But as a novelist and an exotic Black professor who has lived many years abroad, hamming it up is as much a professional stock in trade as it is for a ward politician, and my students love it. Especially my Black students, of which there are only a sprinkling in my classes, with the exception of my Black Lit class, which is made up almost entirely of Black students. At the end of the hour I hadn't had a chance to glance at all of the papers as they were sheepishly turned in, but one paper, turned in after less than fifteen minutes of frantically confident pen-scratching by a fat Black girl, was so cryptic and strange that I read it to myself three times, long after the classroom was deserted.

(This girl she 5'6" tall and has weight of average person, has large Afro on her head, wear a skirt about 3 inches from her knee. Complexion medium brown. Like dark colors. Walk fast always. Wear a black coat with gold button down the front. Appears a very likeable person. Was at one time very active in football, basketball, handball. Like children. Once start something always hope to finish the project. But she only visit your English class. Is always dieting never losing more than a few pounds at a time.

Rainy days are her best day. She hate math. But would like to drive a car or airplane or truck. Has hope of completing her education and traveling around some. Wish to have at least six or seven kids, they are all tax deductible. Not like to get up early in the morning and refuse to go to bed at night. I like this class, but I am not in it officially. Thank you for letting me sit in.)

What did she mean by that: *Not in my class officially?* Was she some kind of spy sent by the Dean—or, even worse, sent to spy on me by the ultra-militant Afro-American Student Union, some of whom have already accused me of being a Negro Bourgeois Lackey for having lived in Europe.

But now I rapped on the door three times as Miss Pariss instructed me to do. And this time the door opened widely, almost before I had finished knocking, and Miss Pariss invited me inside with the nonchalant flourishing gesture of a duchess welcoming a visiting ambassador.

"Come right in, sir," she said, her accent now stilted and cultivated, almost European. "You are right on time—*The Bill Cosby Show* is due to go on the air in just five minutes . . ."

The entrance hall was completely dark and by now there was only a lingering scent of pork fat and greens. But the overwhelming sweet density of incense which permeated the musty air after she carefully secured the locks gave me the odd impression of entering an opium parlour like one I once visited in Macao—an impression enhanced by the tiny pink-shaded boudoir lamps scattered strategically about the living room to create a romantic or funereal atmosphere, and the eerie moving shadows on the TV screen, thc colors of which, due to some long-neglected technical break-down, were predominantly yellows and greens.

"Have a seat, young man," Miss Pariss said graciously, assuming the tone and mannerisms of a TV commercial hostess, "over there on the sofa in front of the Tee Vee—Reverend Grooms, get off your fat lazy ass and get our writer guest a drink!"

Only now did I recognize the shadowy form seated on the far corner of the sagging sofa as the strangely garbed man I had met on the landing while waiting for Miss Pariss to open the door. The console of whistles again wheezed jarringly in his chest, and he cast an evil glance of resentment in my direction as laboriously he hoisted his flabby frame up from the sofa and limped over to a round table, in the very center of the room, covered with a yellow velvet tasseled cloth upon which were lit two candles in altar-like candlesticks and between which were two glasses with likenesses of Martin Luther King and Bobby Kennedy stamped on them, a plastic bowl of ice cubes, a pitcher of water, a huge can of mixed nuts, a freshly-opened bottle of medium-priced scotch whiskey and a nearly half-empty jug of red Gallo wine, no doubt the same jug Reverend Grooms was nursing under his arm when I first encountered him. Now Reverend Grooms was wearing a spotted black suit and a clerical collar at least two sizes too large for his neck, which in spite of his flabby overweight body was strangely skinny like the neck of a hormone-fattened turkey.

Sulkily Reverend Grooms prepared two drinks of scotch and clumsily handed me my drink first, almost spilling it.

"You should have asked our guest if he wanted his straight," Miss Pariss said as she settled down in an armchair draped with a needlepoint effigy of an African warrior, in the heroically contracted pose of a Black Mister America, on the back as a head rest.

"Oh, this will be fine," I said, moving toward the side of the sofa as far from Reverend Grooms as possible, and away from the glare of the TV set, whose wavering yellow and green images were already making me dizzy.

"Well, I want more scotch in mine, Reverend Grooms," Miss Pariss said curtly, "you don't have to be skintchy with *my* scotch . . ."

Stifling a grumbling remark, Reverend Grooms dutifully splashed more scotch in Miss Pariss' glass and handed it to her with exaggerated deference—so much so that I could not help but come to the conclusion that he must function as Miss Pariss' butler. He had just returned to the table and was filling a chipped water glass with red Gallo wine, pausing to gulp down over half the contents of the glass before refilling it, when Miss Pariss shouted:

"The nuts, Reverend Grooms! The nuts! Offer our guest the mixed cocktail nuts—"

"Oh, I've just had dinner," I said hastily. "The drink will be just fine—"

"Well, *I* want some of them mixed cocktail nuts, Reverend Grooms is just being his usual evil self—he knows perfectly well I always have mixed cocktail nuts with my *good* scotch—it enhances the aroma of the malt—I learned that in Edinburgh from a scotch whisky broker who was a great admirer of my talent when I was on one of my European tours—"

"Yeah, I can just imagine what kind of talent of yours he was admiring—"

"Reverend Grooms, you've got a mind that goes swimming every night in the sewers—and you still have the liver gall to call yourself a man of God!"

Reverend Grooms settled back against the sofa and smiled dreamily and took another long drink of wine.

"Girl, we going to miss the beginning of the show with Lola Falana and all them dancing girls prancing around and doing their thing—and I don't want to miss all those cartoons at the beginning either—"

"I don't want to hear you calling me 'girl'—you ain't got no business getting familiar with me around our writer guest!"

"You keep eating all those mixed nuts you're going to end up with your intestines turning into a peanut butter sausage! You know you got regularity trouble as it is—"

"You better get me my mixed nuts, you jackleg wino hypocrite!"

By now *The Bill Cosby Show* was flashing on the screen with all its synthetic jive and super-hip poor-mouth humble ghetto jokes, and the fantastic bedtime sexuality of the dancing girls. *The Bill Cosby Show* is my favorite show business special: I do my best thinking while watching it and find it especially conducive to marking boring student themes while it is on. But that night, in the strangely obsessive presences of Reverend Grooms and Miss Mona Pariss I couldn't keep my eye on the screen. My mind was jumbled with confused misgivings about the interview. How should I approach Miss Mona Pariss' life? Humorously, nostalgically, reverentially—the combined saintliness of Josephine Baker and Bessie Smith? But suddenly now there was dead silence in the room, the abrupt silence of a church when the passing of the collection plate is announced. The show was over and the TV set turned off.

Reverend Grooms broke the silence, shaking his head and cackling with appreciation.

"That Bill Cosby sure puts on a show! Even if he is only a colored boy from South Philly, I say he puts on a better show than Johnny Carson! And that's the gospel truth!"

He had shuffled over to the center table and was pouring himself another glass of wine, his puffy misshapen face relaxed in a smile of complete digestive and libidinous satisfaction.

"You may go now, Reverend Grooms!" Miss Pariss announced imperiously. "And take that jug of wine with you—I simply can't endure the stink of that cheap dago red—!"

Chastized, Reverend Grooms' face melted into a sullen formless pulp. Casting an evil resentful glance in my direction, he defiantly wiped his lips on his sleeve, tucked the jug of wine under his arm, and struggled to walk with dignity toward the door, his thick lips pursed tightly in offended silence. When the door closed behind him, Miss Pariss rose for the first time since my arrival and again performed the meticulous ritual of securing all the locks. Then, smiling coyly, she turned to me and said in a formal yet cute tone of voice:

"And now, sir, shall we begin the interview?"

Suddenly it occurred to me that I neglected to bring a tape recorder. From her initial reaction to the proposed interview I had naturally assumed that my purpose in being invited that evening had been to begin a long period of negotiations as to whether or not she would even consent to be interviewed. But apparently her decision had been made.

"Shall we begin the interview, sir?" she repeated, rising slowly and approaching me with her hands on her hips, with the slow studied undulating walk of a nightclub singer coyly approaching the microphone after the spotlight centers on her figure.

"Why, yes—of course," I stammered, taking a step backwards and almost knocking over one of the pink shaped boudoir lamps set on a fragile corner table.

"But I'm afraid I didn't bring my tape recorder with me. You see, I assumed you would want to discuss the kind of interview the magazine has in mind first—"

"Never mind," she said, her voice lowered to a husky challenge. "I'm sure the interview will go along just perfect. So if you don't mind let's go into the other room where we'll be more comfortable—"

And she picked up the bottle of scotch and our two glasses and led the way through a heavily curtained door opening into a short, cluttered hallway, on one side of which was a tiny kitchen, the door blocked with an overflowing trash can, to still another door, this one also heavily draped with red velvet hangings.

"This is where I do my meditating and futurizing," she said nonchalantly as I followed her through the drapes, finding myself in a huge high-ceilinged room with hand-painted beams, a spacious thick-walled room with a fireplace and glassed-in balcony thick with a jungle growth of plants with huge waxy luxuriant leaves.

The room was at least twice as large as the sitting room we had just left, and even with the canopied bed which dominated the center of the room it gave the impression more of a temple or the chapel of a funeral parlour than of a bedroom.

"This is where I do my meditating and futurizing and my praying exercises," she repeated, as if to emphasize not only the difference of function of the two rooms but the transformation of personality each room apparently enhanced.

There was no overhead lighting, just tiny imitation candle-shaped electric lights set under the figures of plastic saints such as one sees in the Puerto Rican magic medicine shops in my West Side neighborhood, though all the saints' faces had been painted jet black (the blond hair of one saint, however, had been incongruously left painted in bright yellow). The huge canopied bed that dominated the center of the room was covered neatly with a damask bedspread. And on either side of the bed were petite boudoir chairs, they too covered with cheap red velvet. In one corner of the room (there was no other furniture which further contributed to the funeral parlour-temple atmosphere and spaciousness of the room) there was an old-fashioned rolltop desk upon which she placed the bottle of whisky and the two glasses.

"Too late in the night for ice," Miss Pariss said brightly as she began pouring two drinks of straight whisky, filling each of the Martin Luther King–Robert Kennedy memorial chalices nearly half full.

My attention had been drawn to the water-stained wall opposite the draped window upon which were hanging, in random gallery fashion, an incredible number of framed posters and faded glossy photographs of Miss Pariss during many stages of her career. On one very large gilt-framed photograph prominently placed in the center of the display, she was mounted on a huge white horse wearing a floppy garden party hat, a tight-waisted long skirted lace dress, and carrying a parasol. Apparently she wasn't ready yet to discuss the photographs and posters, for she hurried over to where I was standing and prodded me on the arm with the glass of whisky.

"Let us relax first, and gain inner harmony," she said in yet another change of voice, this one the deep-throated voice of an oracle.

Then, holding her own glass in her free hand, she took me

strongly by the hand and led me to one of the chairs beside the enormous canopied bed.

"You sit yourself down and make yourself comfortable," she said, "while I stretch out so I can get my thoughts together—I never could do no meditating or futurizing sitting down or standing up—"

She was staring at me, not exactly directly, but with her eyes half-closed, as if staring at the inside of my mind. But at the same time she was looking at me as a sexually-aroused woman looks at a man. And this was very unnerving, especially in those mumbo-jumbo surroundings. Nervously I took a deep drink from my glass and was about to comment on the photographs to distract her powerful gaze when suddenly she began to giggle:

"This like one of them welfare psychiatrist sessions, ain't it the truth! You sitting there with your notebook and pencil ready to write down what I say and me stretched out here all comfortable and relaxed getting myself together to start memorizing—"

The incense burning somewhere in the room and the whisky were beginning to give me a high, as though I were floating beneath water or in a dream. To regain control of my critical faculties I forced myself to concentrate on the details of her appearance, but I was only able to observe the dress she was wearing, so mockingly intimidating was her powerful gaze. It was a kind of evening gown of faded black satin with fringes around the bosom and halfway down the skirt—a theatrical costume of some long-past era, I decided, making a mental note of the fact.

"You like this dress?" she said, primly pulling down the skirt which had bundled up above her knees when she stretched out on the bed.

"I find it extremely attractive," I said, "a most original creation. Did you make it yourself?"

She laughed so hard she began to choke.

"Of course I didn't make this dress—Reverend Grooms he designed it and made it himself. That wino fool could of made hisself a fortune designing clothes if he hadn't a been born Black and decided to go into the gospel preaching business. That nigger's been designing my clothes for over fifty years! And he ain't no funny-fairy folk either!"

She said this with such earnest conviction and affection that I again had to make a mental note to investigate and reevaluate the relationship between Miss Pariss and Reverend Grooms. But I realized with an ever-deepening sense of dread that my scrupulous schematic approach to this interview would have to be completely cast aside.

For even then I knew that this was no simple human interest story of a long-neglected Black entertainer. Whatever this woman was about it was drenched with the balsam of mystery from which ancient myths derive. And perhaps she sensed the chill of uneasiness that had come over me, for she said, again in her normal (if she indeed had a normal voice) bantering tone:

"I call it my memorizing and meditating dress—I always put it on when I do my meditating and futurizing—"

"Then you agree to the interview?" I said, a bit too eagerly, involuntarily leaning forward as if to settle down to hear a story.

For what seemed an eternity Miss Pariss said nothing and I began to fidget on the edge of the chair.

"Well, I must say I'm very pleased," I said in a cheerfully altered voice. "I think it's safe to tell you that the editor of the magazine even thinks your life is so important to Black History that the interview series may well be expanded into a book!"

Still Miss Pariss said nothing, and continued her relentless staring, making me so nervous that I took a long drink from my glass, knowing well that it was completely empty. At the same time I was beginning to feel slightly drunk, and my eyelids had become so heavy that for a moment of panic I entertained the ridiculous notion that perhaps she was hypnotizing me.

But then, in a tiny secretarial voice that seemed to penetrate my consciousness from some faulty long-distance telephone connection, I heard her saying:

"Yes, indeed, child—my life's a book all right. Course everybody's life is a book, but ain't nobody's life a book like my life's a book—! Yes, child, my life's a book, all right—a holy book, and I don't mean to be sacrilegious!"

Another long pause with the incense-laden silence vibrating with the obsessive bass beat of the hi-fis on the floor below.

"Pour me some more whisky, youngblood!" she ordered almost angrily.

I jumped to my feet as though a whip had been cracked around my neck and rushed to fill her glass which I ceremoniously handed to her as an acolyte serves a priest.

"You pour yourself a drink, too—" she said, her tone now maternal and protective. "If you want to hear the story of my life you've got a lot of listening to do, so you better come right over here on the bed and stretch out comfortable here beside me—"

Then while I was pouring myself yet another drink, my hands shaking, she rose up on her elbow and moved over to the far side of the enormous damask-covered bed.

"Now then—" she said, as I gingerly stretched out alongside

her, biting my lips to fight the sinking feeling of dizziness that was overcoming me from too much to drink. "You just lay there and relax your body and soul. You sure one cute dude for not being one of those funny fairies from downstairs—"

"They nice polite fellows, mind you—" she continued after a thoughtful pause. "Sometimes I invite them up here and tell their fortunes, and tell them the ins and outs of show business when they're out of work—which is most of the time, now that they stopped using colored on the stage in favor of all those long-haired whites twanging their guitars. Cornfield music, we used to call it. But they so mammy hungry they get on my nerves always asking me 'should I do this' or 'should I do that' or 'would I mind sewing a button on their crotches.' Makes me feel old, and while my flesh may not be as young as it used to be, my blood runs as hot as peppermint tea soon as I get a little scotch in me. Yes, Lord! Don't talk to me about no geriatrics! When geriatrics starts heading my way, they won't have to put me in the grave, I'll dive in head first!"

And she laughed so hard I thought she was having a fit. Finally, though, she caught her breath and regained her poise.

"Now if you'll just take off your jacket and make yourself at home, so to speak, we might as well get down to work on this interview of yours—"

I quickly jumped off the bed, overjoyed to be doing something that was at once real and familiar and not something out of a waking nightmare and fumbled for the note pad and pencil in the inside pocket of my jacket.

"While you up," she said, "you might as well take off your clothes—"

"Take off my clothes?" I gasped, turning.

"What's the matter with you, youngblood? Are you sure you ain't one of them funny fairies from downstairs? Don't you understand plain English?"

"You want me to take off my clothes and get in bed with you?"

"You heard what I said. Don't you know what I'm talking about?"

"Do you mean you want me to—er—to—to go to bed with you before you'll give me an interview?"

Again she broke out into that highpitched screaming laugh of hers.

"You been reading my mind, youngblood."

My own forced laughter was at once cautious, involuntary, and forced—gallows laughter. And a spasm of shock and terrified reverence completely paralyzed my thinking.

"But Miss Pariss," I stuttered, averting my eyes, but choosing my words as delicately as I was able.

"But Miss Pariss—" I repeated clumsily. "This is—well, ridiculous, I mean this isn't exactly what I had in mind—"

"You mean you don't want to share my bed with me?"

"I by no means wish to give you the impression that I don't want to share your bed with you. It's only that—"

"Just because you a pretty youngblood dude, you think you too good to share my bed just because you think I'm a senior citizen or one of them geriatric cases—?"

"Believe me, Miss Pariss. We've known each other only a short time, hardly a day—and yet I am convinced you are the most remarkable woman I have ever met—"

But even as the words came out of my mouth I knew that I was only rehearsing the very words I would be repeating to Gracie the next day when inevitably she would ask me how I thought the interview would go. After all, Gracie had her problems with the editorial staff at the fledgling magazine, and she had already told me she was having a very hard time thinking up new ideas for articles that were both "interesting to a large Black mass audience and provocative."

If for no other reason than Gracie's courage and trust in me I had no choice but to go through with the interview no matter what the cost to my personal sensibilities. And besides, I desperately needed the money.

So with the slow stagey motions of a strip-tease artist I began to undress. And when I was down to my leopard skin briefs (the room now completely dark except for a single pink electric candle under a plastic black-faced saint of St. George slaying a dragon) her now deep oracle voice boomed through the fumes of incense and she said in a priestly command:

"Take it off! Take it all off! Ashes to ashes, dust to dust—!"

Then as I sat gingerly on the edge of the bed she took my hand and placed it against the rouged smoothness of her sunken cheek.

"Now don't that feel as soft as a baby's behind?" she said gently.

I felt heat and throbbing blood. And, after what seemed to be an endless moment of mystical anticipation, not unlike the elevation of the mass, she placed her withered hand between my naked legs and let out a glory shout.

"It's up, youngblood, it's up! May the Good Lord be praised! I could tell by that funny slant in your left eye you was some special kind of dude, so now get ready to hear the truth—the true truth, the whole truth, and nothing *but* the truth, straight out of the holy book of the life of Madam Mona Pariss Babu!"

3

When I stole out of Miss Pariss' crumbling brownstone the next morning shortly before dawn, the first sullen muffled Black and Puerto Rican workers were already sleepwalking down the dungeon steps of the 96th Street and Broadway subway station and the usual shivering coterie of winos had already huddled into its wax museum pose of eternal waiting, like cold famished pigeons in the entranceway of the Thalia Theatre next to the corner liquor store waiting for it to open.

My mind was befuddled and I felt ill at ease on the street at that hour of the morning; and, after sidestepping an old Irish woman wearing a medieval costume made up of newspapers and cardboard tied around her body with nylon rope who was muttering to herself that it was time to go to Mass and buy a lottery ticket, I stopped at the corner newsstand to buy *The New York Times*.

Feeling depressed, humiliated and full of hangover misgivings (the eyes of the winos converging on me like blips on a radar screen), I went home to my apartment a few blocks away on

Amsterdam Avenue and took a hot shower and, dropping wearily between the sheets without bothering to wipe myself off, fell almost immediately asleep.

When I awoke, it was eleven-thirty and, on sudden impulse, feeling the desperate need to prod myself out of the ominously destructive mood engendered by my creeping doubts about the interview with Miss Pariss, I decided to phone Gracie at her office, something she absolutely prohibited me from doing in the morning.

Imitating the work habits of a well-publicized New York feminist executive whom she secretly admired, though she would never forgive me if I were to make such a statement to her face, Gracie always shows up at her office at least two hours before any of the others on the staff show up for work in order, as she puts it, "to do my heavy thinking."

When finally her Barbados-accented girl Friday haughtily passed the line, I told her that I absolutely had to talk to her about the Mona Pariss piece.

And, no doubt because my futile attempts to sound poised and confident were hardly sufficient to mask the desperate mood I was in, and mainly perhaps because of the fuzzy incoherence of what I was trying to say—which, I suppose, she attributed to the excitement and enthusiasm for the material I was gathering, she reluctantly agreed to come to my apartment during her lunch hour after pointedly reminding me that there would be no time for "fooling around" as she had a two-thirty editorial conference, and that she could spend at the *very most* forty minutes with me.

I then took another shower, turned on the all-day news program, took a pill to calm my nerves and promptly fell to sleep during an on-the-scene play-by-play report of a bank hold-up in Brooklyn with fifteen welfare recipients who were cashing their checks being held as hostages.

The automatic radio alarm awakened me from some terrifying but immediately erased nightmare having to do with an anthill and a thatched hut, and I hastily dressed in my velvet combat jacket and a new checked shirt and settled down in my most maternally comfortable armchair to try to look over some of those biographical sketches I had afflicted on my Freshman Composition class.

Exactly twenty-seven minutes later (the elevators must have been out of order again and I live on the 28th floor), the doorbell rang and Gracie came rushing into my carpeted cozy retreat (not at all unlike thousands of other carpeted cozy retreats of recently divorced writers), perfumed and still super-charged with downtown energy, a gust of executive storminess, highstrung and breathless.

"Christ! What a shitty wasted morning!" (Her scatological expletives were a chic vestige of her Vassar education.) "Give me a stiff drink and a joint. Those nigger bitches on the staff been acting like they all having their periods on the same day! So naturally it ends up with me having to make all the decisions, do *all* the re-writing—you remember that soul food story *Ebony* ran about three issues ago? Well that bitchy food editor I hired last week wants to run almost exactly the same story with a color spread that will cost at least ten thousand dollars—but with some shitty recipes she said she found in the library about a typical Christmas dinner on a South Carolina plantation during slave days, then run it alongside the recipes of what the slaves would have been eating the same day! I mean *really*—!"

Personally I thought it was a terrific idea, but fortunately I said nothing, knowing all too well that what Gracie was really upset about was that she hadn't thought up the idea first. I let the silence fill itself with our ritualistic inhaling of the joints, until abruptly Gracie glanced at her watch and said, "Well—?"

"Well, what?"

"What happened?"

"Oh, you mean the interview with Mona Pariss?"

"Well, that's what you dragged me up here to talk about, wasn't it? The way you sounded on the phone didn't sound any too good—"

"Gracie! You'll never believe it. She's something else. An absolutely fabulous character. Not only could you run a whole series on her life, but a book—eventually a movie, maybe even a musical!"

"Are you sure you're all right? Cut out all the bullshit and tell me what *really* happened!"

I was thinking of the thousand-dollar advance which I needed desperately to appease the threatening letters I had been receiving from my Master Charge account. My expression must have frozen into abject panic.

"All right," she said in an altered, almost kindly, tone of voice calculated to aid my descent into a cool Manhattan business world acceptance of failure. "What happened? And none of your novelist bullshit. Do we or do we not have a story?"

"Do we have a story?" I shouted, leaping to my feet and almost literally prancing around the room. "Do we have a story? Why this woman's life is a book, a holy book—"

"A holy what?"

"What I mean is her whole life is a metaphor for the universal initiation myth—"

"Edwards, look. I like you. I like you in bed. I love the way you write. But your thinking is fuzzy and what you're saying is pure unadulterated intellectual nigger jive! I'm not interested in a book—least of all a holy book, and our readers could care less about a metaphor for an initiation myth. You forget this magazine is called *New Black Woman* and most of our readers have been initiated by the time they were nine years old. What the magazine really needs is—as I've told you at least a thousand times—is a nice inspiring article about a forgotten Black artist like 'The Lady Sings the Blues,' only more upbeat without all the oppression and drugs . . ."

I choked on an overly deep draw of marijuana smoke (cursing the seeds and the dealer who sold me the inferior stuff), and while I was coughing convulsively, something in the wild look in my eyes must have alerted Gracie to my true state of frantic agitation.

"Look," she said quietly, again stealing a glance at her watch like a station master about to raise his signal panel, "I have exactly ten minutes. Now, for Christ's sake, will you please tell me what in the hell happened?"

I have known Gracie too long to fool her. We have been lovers on and off for almost ten years, both before and after our divorces. So I had no choice but to tell her the truth.

"She made me lay in bed with her!"

"She *what—?*"

"She made me lay in bed with her—otherwise she wouldn't consent to the interview!"

"Are you out of your mind or on some kind of trip? That woman must be pushing ninety. You mean you actually went to bed with a ninety-year-old woman?"

"Gracie—promise you'll never tell anyone—"

"Tell anybody what?"

"That I have to lay in bed with Miss Pariss every time I visit her before she'll tell me her life story—"

Gracie laughed so loud and hysterically that I broke out into a cold sweat.

Since becoming a Manhattan magazine executive, Gracie seldom laughs during office hours, so I was justifiably alarmed. Finally she stopped laughing and tenderly placed an arm around my shoulder, and this alarmed me even more.

"You know something," she said, gently, almost compassionately, "when I first thought of you for this assignment, I was almost sure something weird would come out of it. I mean, you've got a freakish mind and people like you attract weird happenings like a magnet. But this—! This is not only weird it's beautiful, Gothic, I mean, not even a novelist could invent a story like this—"

"Gracie, that's what I'm supposed to be—a novelist—"

"I know you're a novelist—and a fairly good one, and that's why I thought of you for this assignment. But even *you* wouldn't put a thing like this in a novel. No one would believe it—What was it like?"

I was sinking into an ugly resentful mood. I pushed her arm off my shoulder and sprawled sulkingly in my corner armchair.

"What was *what* like?"

"You know what I mean. What was it like going to bed with a ninety-year-old woman?"

"She's not ninety years old—she could pass for fifty."

But I could tell by the almost childish tone of her voice that Gracie really was interested in something she had never thought of before—like a young girl asking a close girl friend who had just had her first affair with a man what it was like. In Gracie's expression was the avid curiosity of a little girl asking her first tentative questions about the mystery of sex, the reverential appealing look of one of my freshman students asking the meaning of some esoteric line of modern poetry.

Suddenly our roles had reversed. I had power over Gracie; I had become suddenly endowed with an aura of almost priestly magic. So how really could I tell her that I hadn't had to make love to Miss Pariss—only stretch out under the covers with her so that our spirits could communicate freely as we slept or talked so that whenever anything came to her mind, either in a dream, or by the free association of our conversation, I could at once make a note of it? Deciding on the more ambiguous course of letting Gracie's imagination travel in whatever direction it chose, I said with the quiet professional sincerity of a minister having a quiet tea in his study with one of his more troubled parishioners:

"Gracie, it's not what it was *like* that is important—but that Miss Pariss finds it absolutely necessary to establish this manner of communion every time I go to interview her. She is somewhat of a believer in occult subjects—not a nut or a fanatic, don't misunderstand me—more of a primitive psychologist, a most fascinating intelligent woman. Lying in bed together—it's the only way she'll tell me her life story—"

Gracie's imagination had been traveling with such frantic speed that I was certain she hadn't heard a word I said. Gazing into my eyes longingly as though I had had the privilege of participating in some mysterious ritual never before participated in by anyone she had ever known, she asked breathlessly:

"For example—" her expression even more childlike (Manhattan tough executive girl Gracie!), her whole body arched rigidly toward me as though impatient to hear the denouement of a familiar fairytale, "—I mean, for example, is her pubic hair white?"

If I told her that I had no way of knowing, the room having been immersed in almost total darkness, or that I had had no interest in glancing even furtively at that part of her body, which at any rate was covered by that outlandishly red petticoat she was wearing, Gracie might have recovered her cool enough to think I was putting her on. On the other hand, I had to keep her interest sustained at this mesmerized intensity at least long enough to approach the subject of money.

"Miss Mona Pariss is all woman—" I said mysteriously, folding my hands in an attitude of prayer. "So let's leave it at that—shall we?"

Gracie was growing angry and frustrated and ashamed of her momentary loss of sophistication; I could tell by the way she was scraping both feet on the floor in time to some inaudible rhythm and blues.

"All woman—!" She snorted contemptuously, "—now what in the hell is that supposed to mean? Here you are supposed to be a novelist, a poet, a professor, a thinker—and all you come up with is some cracker barrel comment like 'Miss Pariss is all woman!'"

"Well, let me try to put it like this—"

I hadn't the slightest idea what I was going to say, so even I was surprised by the sheer poetry of the words that rushed out of my mouth:

"Imagine going to a place far out in the bush, somewhere in Africa, let's say—to a lonely isolated hut, no trees, only anthills as high as McDonald's hamburger joints—"

(Only then did I realize that the nightmare was coming back to haunt my memory from the darkened screening room where it had been lurking in wait for an appropriate audience all the time.)

"And in the hut there is an old woman, an old wrinkled woman, hundreds of years old, a wise woman, a seer, a prophetess—and I humbly enter the hut and ask for a drink of water, a supplicant—I have come millions of miles over the desert of time with a riddle, I must know the answer, and the old prophetess tells me she will only give me the answer, the meaning of the riddle, if I make love to her—"

Gracie is frightened, I can tell by her frozen expression and flickering eyelids—that either what I have just said or the hallucinated cadence of my saying it, the reverberating vestige of my own terrified sense of mystery about everything that happened the night before, has transformed what for her was an amusingly sophisticated fairytale—a story to be repeated over cocktails at some mid-town pseudo-continental literary luncheon—into a death-laden ancestor cult African ghost story. So, quickly I shifted emotional gears and broke out into a brittle laugh.

"Oh—and I forgot to tell you—there's another weird character on the scene—a certain Reverend Grooms, someone you'd have to see to believe—"

"Well, where does he fit into the picture? I'm only interested in Mona Pariss and her career—you can save the freak show for your next novel—"

"I don't know yet—" I said honestly, adding for no particular reason, "He drinks red Gallo wine—"

"Edwards, you're a nut, but I love you—"

She again looked at her watch and jumped to her feet and rushed for the door.

"That joint has made me feel horny as hell—I better get out of here—!"

Thank God, Gracie was back in a good or at least charitable mood again.

"Then you think we've got the makings of a great series of articles?" I asked, still not daring to approach the subject of a second supplementary advance.

"Baby, I trust you—I may be a fool, but I trust you. But if you fuck up on this assignment you're going to be number one on my shit list—and I'll loudmouth you all over New York so that you won't even be able to get a writing job as a welfare case worker—!"

The door slammed in my face before I could kiss her goodbye, and I knew that she meant exactly what she said, and I turned up the radio to drown out any possibility of thinking about the obsessive nightmare this Mona Pariss assignment had by now become.

4

The next day could only be described as Black Wednesday.

Possibly because of my insane paranoia about my next interview with Miss Pariss, a meeting I both feared and yet strangely anticipated, not unlike the fear and chilling anticipation a child experiences boarding the toy train for a ride through a tunnel of horrors, I was by no means in top form for my teaching chores (adding to my state of inner toil was the fact that two days had passed since Gracie had come to my apartment and the check she had promised in a later telephone call still had not arrived, while various credit bureau thugs had been suggesting that I pay up or else), and for the first time since I began my teaching career, I let my Black Lit class get out of control. Or perhaps explode into a riot is a more accurate description of what happened.

There are about twenty-four students in the class. Only two are white—an earnest pimply Irish Catholic young man whose four brothers have all entered the religious life in one form or the other while he himself (as he soon informed me) aspires to a career as a radical urban social worker, and a very neurotic Jewish girl who had shared a Lower East Side pad with a Black musician and whose mother had had a passionate love affair with a Black civil rights activist during the Freedom Rides of the 1960s. Among the Black students are several West Indians with their use of "proper English, colonial-style" as opposed to the uninhibited ghetto street English the Brooklyn and Harlem students defiantly affect in class discussions, and of course their somewhat smug West Indian awareness of a longer tradition of "Black Consciousness."

There are, making up the larger portion of the class, mild sheltered Black girls from Staten Island whose political outlook reflects the arch conservative values of the white Staten high schools they attended, values which clothe their thinking like prim Sunday church-going frocks—and, of course, the hulking cynical street Blacks, aspirant professional basketball stars or cool hustlers (on the surface at least, for most of them have sharp probing minds which makes challenging them with advanced intellectual concepts such a gratifying teaching experience: which I suppose is what I mean when I mentioned the perverse joys of classroom pomposity and hamming it up, the delightful show-business side to teaching). And there is the devil incarnate herself, Melinda Rodriguez—fiery Puerto Rican nationalist and self-styled revolutionary, sexy as an ascetic nun turned call girl, who contemptuously informed me the first day of class that she was only taking the course to work off her English Literature requirements, preferring Black Lit to a course on Milton, the only other course with the same time slot that would free her for her afternoon job with the Socialist Workers Party.

For the first two classes she sat in the front row directly in front of me with such a look of devastating contempt on her pretty little face that, in spite of all my efforts to be cool and academically noncommittal in my introductory lectures (I would work up a more militant Black nationalist stance later if the situation required, never quite knowing at the beginning of the semester where my students' heads were or what the current political fads were: I remember one semester, two years ago, a group of four students showed up in class wearing obviously homemade "Arab" robes and Hindu turbans), I found myself adjusting my remarks directly to her instead of to the class in general—almost translating my thoughts for her with the inevitable loss of any coherent development of what I thought were original ideas about the long historical conflict between art, politics and race consciousness in Black writing in the United States.

At any rate, I was in the midst of a rambling elucidation of Richard Wright's early perception of America's institutionalized racism, which, as he painfully discovered, had even infected liberal supporters of Black causes and even the Communist Party itself, and his even more relevant identification of a new and restlessly alienated type of urbanized humanity, a waste product of highly industrial societies undergoing speeded-up social and technological change, the vast multitudes of Bigger Thomases lost and adrift, desperately seeking identities who would erupt into senseless acts of violence until provided with macabre uniforms and emblems and charismatic leaders on horseback to follow like lemmings to the edge of the abyss.

"What the fuck do you know about institutionalized racism?" Miss Rodriguez shouted suddenly in the midst of my erudite analysis.

"And who gives a fuck about the Jews in Nazi Germany or the white racist ethnics of the Depression years. And anyway who gives you the right to be talking about racism and social dynamics in the first place? Christ, you're an associate professor of English, right? In the City System—a nice easy clean job that pays you at least twenty thousand a year. Right? Look at you! You've got it made. Look at those fucking pimp clothes you wear. You spend your summers loafing around Europe. You call yourself Black but you've already sold yourself out to the American Dream—a pocketful of credit cards, a flashy car. The only thing Black about you are those creepy black boots you're wearing trying to convince us you're really a hip swinger at heart. You're a jive nigger, man—pure unadulterated jive and what you're saying about this Richard Wright is about as relevant to what's happening today as the Chiquita Banana commercial is to a bunch of starving migrant worker kids singing 'Jesus Loves Me, Yes I Know, for the Bible Tells Me So'—!"

And she didn't stop there. Whatever pills she had been taking that morning were mighty potent, for her pretty face had become the face of a fury as she looked around the bearbaiting giggling class and rose to new heights of invective, as by now the laughter and catcalls had become a rousing Sousa march of derisive support.

"You know how much my old man used to make before he turned himself in to the Veterans' Hospital? Less than one fifth of what you make, and you know how many kids he had to raise on that crummy salary? Six kids. Six mouths to feed! Sure the Blacks have suffered—but who the hell ever talks about Puerto Ricans and how we suffer? This is a dog-eat-dog society, man! A jungle society where you better grow sharp teeth and sharper claws and carry an even sharper knife and get your hands on some of the white man's guns. Because that's what it's all about, man! Revolution! Total revolution! And they only pay you to go to a crummy college like this because the Establishment's computers and think tanks have figured out that it's cheaper to keep a nigger or a spic in college or the army than keep him in jail! So what's such a big deal about all this bullshit about institutional racism. This Richard Wright whoever he is must be a writer of fairytales like you, that are supposed to give us the illusion of learning some heavy philosophical oatmeal that's really laced with the latest tranquilizer drug invented by the oppressor. If you ask me, neither you nor Richard Wright know your ass from a hole in the ground—you're both a couple of jive turkey nigger cultural sell-outs . . . !"

There was silence and all eyes converged on me and all I could think of to say was almost ludicrously inadequate.

In an almost inaudible voice, really a whisper, so tremendous was my feeling of humiliation and jelly-rollishness before such a storm wind of outrage and anger, I said:

"The times are too urgent, too dangerous and perilous for us all, the apocalypse is here, and the times require serious thought, not sloganizing, and that's exactly why we're here . . ."

Fortunately I was saved by the bell, and the class filed out silently, studiously avoiding my eyes, which were perilously close to tears, and I resisted the temptation to ask Melinda Rodriguez to stay a moment after class.

Instead I sat at my desk trying to calm myself for the next class in Medieval Lit—Chaucer, *The Knight's Tale*, in which I would discuss the origins in chivalry and the Madonna cult of contemporary notions of romantic love.

But first I had to go to the faculty toilet, and as I passed the office of the Black Student Union I could hear raucous hilarious laughter which abruptly stopped as I slunk past like a flea-bitten dog with its tail between its legs.

5

My next interview with Miss Pariss took place the following night, after my spirits had been lifted and the shattering damage to my fragile ego been repaired by the unexpected arrival of a check from Gracie's office, which I almost literally raced to the bank to deposit.

Thus, my financial woes momentarily cast aside, I was in a whistling elated mood as, athletically, I skipped up the dark steps and knocked at Miss Pariss' door.

But instead of Miss Pariss' door opening, the door to Reverend Grooms' apartment banged open as if there had been a gas explosion inside. And I turned just in time to find myself face to face with a drunken enraged apparition wearing torn and faded long woolen underwear, brandishing a knob-headed walking cane at me in one hand and threatening me with a butcher knife with the other.

More than merely drunk, his bloodshot eyes and twisted facial muscles left no doubt in my mind that I was about to be attacked, perhaps even murdered, without the benefit of prayers or the slightest possibility of neighbors rushing to my support. I even read the tiny four-line report in the next day's *Daily News*: "NEGRO COLLEGE PROFESSOR AND NOVELIST SLAIN IN MUGGING INCIDENT ON UPPER WEST SIDE."

"Reverend Grooms!" I said in a tremulous voice, backing to the farthest and darkest corner of the odorous landing. "Are you feeling all right?"

"You cheap two-bit pimp!" he shrieked, the butcher knife and cane slashing the half-darkness of the landing in some intricate parabolic pattern as though he were performing a kind of sword dance.

"You iniquitous disciple of the devil! You youngblood *Super Fly* dude—pimping on a fine Christian woman old enough to be your grandmother! I ought to cut your evil parts and feed them to the hogs!"

"Reverend Grooms—calm down—that butcher knife is dangerous!"

"I may be old and feeble but this butcher knife is a powerful equalizer, you low-down street pimp—calling yourself an educated colored man and a professor—!"

"Reverend Grooms—!"

"Don't you Reverend Grooms me! You haven't the right to speak forth my name—!"

"Sir, perhaps you've had a bit too much to drink. If you'll just calm down I can explain—"

"Explain what?" a peremptory voice behind me said.

Miss Pariss had come to the rescue, and Reverend Grooms slinked back into his door like a vampire suddenly exposed to cloves of garlic, a crucifix and blinding morning light.

"Good evening, Mr. Edwards," Miss Pariss said as though nothing unusual had transpired. "Won't you come in—the reason I couldn't come right away when I heard you knock was I was in the bathroom performing my absolutions. Come in! Come in!"

I slipped hastily into the sanctuary of her apartment, after casting a glance over my shoulder and catching a fleeting strobe light vision of Reverend Grooms' murderous bloodshot eyes stabbing at me through a crack in his door which he hadn't completely closed, the better to overhear our conversation.

"Reverend Grooms' outrageous behavior," Miss Pariss said, as soon as we were seated with our drinks in hand, "must be interpreted in the light of the fact that the poor old fool is desperately in love with me, and has been in love with me since 1923—at least I think that's the year he proposed marriage on the Ferris wheel in Atlantic City where I was appearing in the Boardwalk Frolics—a marriage which for professional reasons and his having been gassed in World War I, I under no circumstances could accept or even contemplate, though there is an enduring bond of affection between us—the old wino bum—and he did make the most fantastic costumes for me, far more original and artistic than those rags Josephine Baker used to wear when she wasn't appearing naked or wearing monkey fruit—So you must not judge Reverend Grooms' expressions of jealous passion too harshly, after all you are a novelist and a man of the world as well as a college professor, and a cute dude yourself with who knows how many women running after you all hours of the night—!"

As soon as we finished the drinks Miss Pariss suggested we go straight to bed and begin our memorializing.

"There's so much to tell. I've been thinking about my life experience all day—and to tell you the truth, I didn't eat a bite all day except two Hershey bars, I was so excited about getting started working on the holy book of my life—"

So in less than twenty minutes after that insane attack on my life I found myself once again stretched out under the covers in the incense-laden darkness of Mona Pariss' futurizing temple, ready to listen and take notes while continuously telling myself all this was reality and I wasn't afloat in some transmigratory nightmare.

"Mr. Edwards," she said, after a scotch-sipping silence that lasted so long I thought she had fallen asleep, "you want the story of my life—and I am sure you are aware that the real problem is how to begin—"

"That, I might add, Miss Pariss, is the novelist's problem as well—"

"Yeah, honey, but this ain't no novel—this is my life, the holy book of my life—"

"But suppose this *were* a novel, and not just the story of your life, your career as one of the greatest Black entertainers of our time—Where would *you* begin?"

"I wouldn't begin the day I was born—that's for sure—and I wouldn't begin the day my daddy and my mother did their thing in bed either—that's not when lives begin—lives begin when you wake up out of that sleep world ghosts live in and you start to move with your own mind and not the mind of a ghost, that's when lives begin—"

"Well, I must say that's very interesting, Miss Pariss—and yet, obviously, we have to begin somewhere. To paraphrase your remarks, when did you wake up out of the sleep world where ghosts live and begin to move with a mind of your own and not the mind of a ghost?"

"That's a long story, youngblood—a long story, so if that's where we're going to begin, you better get off your butt and bring that bottle of scotch over here on the table beside the bed, cause we're both going to need it—and while you're at it, pour a few drops on the floor to sweeten up my memorizing capacities and appease the ghosts of our ancestors that control what we call our earthly lives . . ."

Astonished and intrigued by this social anthropological offhand reference to appeasing the ghosts of our ancestors, I was nevertheless determined not to be sidetracked into any rash intellectual assumptions. After all, this series of articles on Mona Pariss was, in Gracie's hardheaded business-oriented drive for mass circulation, aimed at a vast audience of upward mobile Black housewives more concerned about finding their Black identity in the rosy consumer-oriented American Dream than in any terrifying reminders of a "barbaric" ritual past; so I decided to begin my interview with the most banal talk-show-type question that popped into my mind:

"Just to get started, Miss Pariss," I said, "let me ask you the one question that tens of thousands of our readers are eager to know about. Just how did you get into show business?"

"How I got started in showbiz? Well, youngblood, that's a book in itself, and not the holy book I be talking about—"

And she laughed, almost girlishly, her eyes half-closed and flickering:

"You see, youngblood—it ain't how I got into showbiz, it's how showbiz got into me. When I was a teeny little girl, but not so teeny the mens didn't undress me with their sanctimonious lecherous eyes, down home in Orlando County, a little cotton-field town stuck in the middle of a spooky pine woods—peanut country—well, I used to sing in the church choir, up front—you know, wearing robes that wouldn't hide a peach from a possum, and knowing I was the prettiest girl not only in the choir but in all Orlando County, even though I was only fifteen going on sixteen. You can tell it to the world, youngblood, in those days when I was living down home, I was the prettiest cuddle-up doll the good Lord ever turned out in His heavenly toyshop. I was a sweet little sugar plum, and I knew it, and all the menfolks knew it, and the womens, they knew it too, but there wasn't a thing they could do about it but smile and scrinch their eyes shut like they was praying instead of cursing me under their breath. . . .

"Well, down home in those days in Orlando County they used to have what was called Christian Gospel Fellowship Week, when all the gospel choirs in the backwoods churches—maybe ten or fifteen from as far as fifty miles around—would all come to town in wagons and trains, and there would be a whole week of gospel singing competition, big chicken and potato salad picnics on a long plank table outdoors, cause it always took place in August just before peanut picking time, and the best choir always got to hang the red and gold Christian Gospel Fellowship Banner behind the pulpit in their church until the next competition the following year. . . .

"Lordy me, I used to love those Fellowship meetings, because you'd get all kinds of people coming back home, from Ohio, even Chicago some of them, and naturally every preacher would be trying to show off his choir the best.

"Well, that year our choir we got all dolled up in gold and white robes—and I tell you, youngblood, I looked like an angel,

I felt like an angel, and I was so overflowing with the Holy Spirit, and feeling so tingly and holy you couldn't even call it singing what I was doing, it was more like being a radio for the voice of the Lord—I'm telling you, I *was* an angel, and if it wasn't for those heavy white and gold robes and those clodhopper shoes we country girls wore back in those days down home, I'd be off *flying* like an angel—

"So, as I was saying—sweeten up my drink, youngblood—as I was saying, to make a long story short, there was a nice-looking light-skinned fellow with good hair I used to go to school with named Doc cause he always used to wear a cute little goatee and keep it Brilliantined all the time, but Doc he dropped out of school and left town telling everybody he was going North because he didn't want to be stuck in no two-bit peanut growing town for the rest of his nigger days, so he finally ended up getting a job as a Pullman porter because of his good looks and his smooth talking and Brilliantined goatee so white folks knew he wasn't no surly trouble-making ugly nigger liable to spit in their food, so to make a long story short, every now and then, maybe twice a year, he'd show up in town togged out in his latest Harlem togs and wearing two or three of those biggy pawnshop rings on his fingers, and he kept his nails long like a Chinaman, like he was always holding a cup of tea in his hand. I mean, he was a smart dresser, elegant like a prince, always talking that latest Harlem jive—and being a Pullman porter and all and a natural-born ladies' man, he naturally had nice manners for all the nice old church ladies and, as I said, a crooning kind of sweet talk that would melt butter on the top of an iceberg in the North Pole—

"Well, as I keep saying, to make a long story short, that summer at the Gospel Fellowship Week meeting he showed up all dolled up in a white suit and a white fedora even though it was so hot even the dogs were too suffocating from the heat to do their regular dog day duties. And when the ladies in our choir was on stage, there he was standing there—not sitting on the benches like everybody else, mind you—but standing there in the front row staring at me and smiling and winking and flashing his pawnshop rings and getting me so nervous and my nature up I almost lost my cue when it was time to do my solo. I always did know he had a sweet tooth for me, but right there in front of all those peoples, everybody could tell what was on that sly mind of his, especially those jealous frumpy ladies in the choir who didn't even bother to keep their eyes scrinched shut like they was communicating with the Spirit, but kept watching us like we was desecrating the holiness of the occasion. And finally even the preacher, he stopped thinking about the collection plate long enough to realize that a snake had entered the Garden of Eden and was slinking around plotting to take away one of his angels—

"And so after we was packing up our robes for the night, the preacher—a goodlooking dude hisself, Preacher Gore I think his name was, with a tiny diamond in his middle gold tooth, well, he comes over to me behind the tent and starts warning me of the way the devil appears in strange disguises, and if I had one hundredth the sense and experience I got now I would've known any preacher with a diamond in his middle gold tooth should have first-hand knowledge about the strange disguises the devil appears in, cause all those pious frisky ladies weren't spending all those nights practicing in the choir just to be singing a new song unto the Lord, no sacreligion meant—I'll have another little taste if you will be so kind, Mr. Edwards—"

And she wiggled her slight petticoated body into an arc-like position and proceeded to emit a series of sonorous farts, so authoritative and prolonged that one was somehow reminded of the lunch hour whistle of the steel mills in Pittsburgh where I was born.

"Thank you kindly, Mr. Edwards," she continued, a wheezing sign celebrating her intestinal tract's jubilant relief.

"Now what was I memorializing about? Oh, yes—how I got into showbiz.

"Well, when the jackleg preacher with the diamond stuck smack in the middle of his middle gold tooth started breathing on me hard in the darkness back of that gospel tent, telling me that the devil appears in mysterious disguises, I thinks now he's about to play one of his laying on of hands sacraments with me like he do with some of those other ugly ladies in the choir. It just never occurred to me that he was warning me about that beautiful dude. Doc. I never would've associated Doc with no devil anyhow—if anything I would have let him come stealing into my sinful dreams like one of them movie-star princes. . . .

"But that Doc, he was something else—I mean he was *fast*! As it happened that night, all us younger girls, we slept in a peanut warehouse which the Goober Peanut Company let the church committee use as a kind of dormitory, so long about midnight I hear this whistling outside the window and I kind of know even though I'm floating off somewhere in a dream that it was Doc whistling out there under the moon, and anyway I couldn't sleep even though I was dreaming on account of being so young with all that hot blood churning me into buttermilk. So I gets off the cot and goes to the window, and there he is standing out there in his white suit and Brilliantined goatee with the full moon shining down upon him just like he was the angel of the Lord, and when he motions for me to come on out, well, I just slipped into my dress like I was a sleepwalker or a zombie and snuck out of that peanut warehouse like it was all a part of the dream. And the first thing you know, there we are loving it up in the bushes down by the river—I don't mean intercoursing, I'll tell you about that later, but just hugging and kissing and loving it up like in a nice clean movie. And that was the first time I'd been with a man, and as far as I was concerned that was what being with a man meant, just lying there in the bulrushes hugging and kissing like Cleopatra and the Prophet Moses. . . .

"Well, sir, toward morning, when those mists was coming over the river and turning all pink and golden with the rising of the sun, I turned over and saw Doc lying there like a sleeping prince and I woke him up and told him I wanted some more hugging and kissing, that I was now ready for the real nitty-gritty—

"When I said that I could tell he was thinking and meditating about what I said and staring at me like he was trying to figure me out, so I just kind of laid there resting and listening to the birds twittle, waiting until whatever he was thinking about would come manifest in his mind. So, finally he told me this weird story about how he never did it with girls, and that a young girl like me would be better off staying a virgin all her life, that way she would be like a priestess and have power over men instead of men having power over her.

"Then after I lay there and let that sink in wondering what he talking about but believing every word of what he saying because of him being such a gentleman and a traveling man who knows the world, he finally turn to me and say: 'Little Angel, you got the sweetest singing voice this side of heaven, and I'm going to take you with me and be your manager, because I'm tired of being a Pullman porter and we both special people with a touch of the ghost world kings in our veins. Sweet little singing angel, you going to come away with me and leave this peanut plantation forever—'

"Now as I tell you, I weren't quite sixteen years old yet, but I had a feeling about things, I mean I could futurize even then, I had this gift of visionizing the future, and even though I felt my religion deep, I know that what I was about to do was the Lord's Will, and that He had sent Doc as His agent and His instrument of fulfilling my life's work, and freeing me so I could go about doing it—and, to make a long story short, I went to the railroad station with him before the sun was fully up so we could catch the morning express train on its northern run as far as the junction, then he hid me in the linen room of one of them fancy parlour cars they had back in those days, and I tell you I traveled on that luxury train North, all the way to Cincinnati—and those colored porters, they brought me food, the finest food I ever ate in my life, on a silver tray with linen napkins just like they served the white folks, and he told all the other porters that I was his cousin and that he was taking me up North to school to be educated.

"Now whether they believed him or not I guess really don't make no difference, I still don't know, but they sure treated me like royalty and I been treated like royalty ever since the rest of my life, and when the train laid over in one of them soup can towns down in Georgia, I forget the name, Doc got off the train and bought me some decent clothes and underwear and stockings, you know—city folk clothes, and when I put them on after he let me slip into the white ladies' washroom with his passkey so I could look at myself in the mirror after everybody else had got off in Cincinnati. Lord, I tell you I looked like just a beautiful Black princess in one of them Walt Disney fairytales—

"But that don't tell you how I actually got into the business, now do it? Well, youngblood, I'll get around to that in a minute. But first let me tell you about Pullman porters. In those days—if you'll pardon the digression—Pullman porters were smart and sophisticated like Black movie stars today, you know—like Sidney Poitier, for example, or Flip Wilson, though I don't like it when he do that Geraldine act in front of white folks, my personal preference is for Bill Cosby.

"So, as I was saying, when Doc he take me to Miss Hendley's Boarding House and he tell her to give me a fine decent room because I was his cousin and that I was going up North to go to school in Cincinnati, I'm sure not one of them Pullman porters believed a word of it, they just figured Doc was setting himself up to make a hustle on the side, they just acted like true gentlemen and played along with the game and no questions asked.

"And the first thing I knew there I was all set up in a fine room with running water and embroidery on the furniture and a picture of Booker T. Washington on one wall and a picture of some pretty cows grazing on the side of a mountain in Switzerland—a room all to myself, the first time in my life, and the good thing about it was that most the other guests in the boarding house was Pullman porters like Doc, all of them treating me like royalty and always complimenting me on my good looks, and no lewd hinting around or trying to rub up against me in the hall, and I'd sing for them sometimes after dinner, and Mrs. Hendley herself would accompany me on the piano, she being a church woman and a part-time *chanteuse* herself. I'm telling you, those were happy days, and I never did regret leaving my family and I didn't even miss singing in the church choir, mostly because of old Preacher Gore's diamond sticking in the middle of his gold tooth and him warning me about the ways of the devil when everybody in the choir knew what he was up to with some of them frisky choir ladies—

"But in every Garden of Eden there always comes a serpent to mess up everything, and in this case that old serpent turned out to be none other than that nice little old yellow lady Mrs. Hendley herself. This is what happened. You see, those Pullman porters would be in town on every Thursday and every Monday—the other days they were either on the road or took a day off in New York or Chicago. So naturally I was by myself most of the time with a lot of time on my hands, though I helped some around the house with the chores, because that's the way my daddy brought us chilluns up. Besides, I was too scared to go outside much with all the fire wagons and horses and people cutting each other up, so most of the time I just hung around the house helping Mrs. Hendley polish the silver and learning embroidery, things like that, so we came to be pretty good friends. Until one day when I was helping her with the ironing, she just ups and says 'Mona, now you tell me the truth—you ain't no cousin of Doc's, is you?'

"Well, the way she ask me, all smiling like the serpent, wearing false eyelashes and lipstick, all winking and crooning like, I figger she must know something, but I just stood there looking down at the double-eagle pattern in her rug. But then she ask me *again*, and when I still don't answer her one way or the other she tell me not to be afraid, that she been around even though she be a church woman herself, and that she could well understand how a young pretty girl like me could be sweet talked into leaving home by a smooth operator like Doc. And she tells me that I don't have nothing to worry about, but that being so good looking and with a sweet singing voice like I got, I could do a lot better for myself than just being the plaything of a common Pullman porter. And she says I ought to start thinking about making a career for myself. . . .

"Well, to make a long story short, she stopped what she was doing right then and there and took me to the piano and taught me a couple of them ragtime tunes, I forget the name of all of them except one called 'The Train Came By but It Didn't Stop,' a number she said was just made to order for me because of Doc and all. And she taught me to sing it and swivel my hips and roll my eyes like the words had double intender meanings, you know what I mean—just a little more scotch, youngblood—You's a real gentleman, kind of remind me of Doc a little bit the way your left eye slants kind of wicked like . . .

"Well anyway, the next day, after I had the song down pat along with five or six other songs, mostly whitefolk songs, she sent for a white foreign gentleman I forget his name, Karias or something like that, a little skinny man with a waxed mustache and a cigar and fluttery hands, and she had him listen to me sing, and she told me that this man and she, Mrs. Hendley, was going to be my managers, and that I could forget all about Doc, and they got me this job singing in a white luncheon club in the financial district where rich businessmen would patronize and do business, peanuts and cotton and farm machinery, big business, you can well imagine, and I tell you I was a hit the first time I opened my mouth, and there was one old white-haired man even gave me a fifty-dollar tip and said he wanted me to go home with him and there were more fifty-dollar bills where that came from, but I told him I was a virgin and that I intended to stay a virgin, and whether you want to believe it or not, I been a virgin my whole life ever since. And that's how I got into show business—"

"What about Doc?" I asked nervously, strangely uneasy about this mysterious emphasis on virginity, haunting images of nuns, priestess cults, oracles parading disturbingly through my mind.

"Well, that's a sad and tragic tale, and I guess I'm to blame as much as anybody, though I couldn't do anything about it, even if I tried. What happened was, I was singing at this rich man's luncheon club days and at night at a private rich folks club, one of those candlelight places and waiters slinking around in tuxedos like undertakers. I'd been there about two weeks, and making quite a name for myself, 'The Black Angel with the Golden Voice' was the way they billed me, and what with the tips and all I was making more money in one night than half the darkies in Orlando County down home made peanut picking in a week, and that was even counting the percentage I had to hand over to Miss Hendley and the foreign gentleman—

"Then one night I was singing the white gentlemen's favorite number, a gospel song I kind of ragtimed up called 'How Far, How Far to Heaven' when all of a sudden I hear a commotion way in the back of the room, and the first thing I know here comes Doc staggering stinking drunk through the tables fighting off the colored waiters trying to pull him back toward the entrance. I mean he looked bad—all red-eyed and raggedy and dirt all over his pants, and right there in the middle of the song, in front of all those white gentlemens he comes up and starts tugging on me and crying a regular Niagara Falls of tears and yelling at the top of his voice that I was his and he wanted me back, screaming that they kidnapped me like back in slavery days, that I was *his* angel and that he couldn't live without me—I tell you I was scared out of my wits and ashamed and feeling sorry for him at the same time, and I almost vomit right there in front of everyone, being as many a night I lay in bed crying myself to sleep because he was homefolks to me and I loved him so, until Miss Hendley she moved me to another rooming house run by a relative of hers and told me I wasn't supposed to see that no-good nigger no more cause he would exploit me and turn me into a streetwalker or worse, singing for beer and pretzels in little honky tonky joints—

"Well, for a while there all those white gentlemens, bankers and businessmen and their lady folks, just looked on and laughed like we was putting on some kind of coon show, but Doc he kept on screaming and carrying on so, calling them white gentlemens terrible curse names and worse and insulting them, repeating over and over again like he was speaking in tongues, screaming and spitting at them, yelling that they was leading me into slavery and other crazy nonsense like that until finally someone called the police and the first thing I knew about fifty beefy white cops was cracking down on Doc's head something terrible—I mean, they beat that poor nigger to a pulp while all the white gentlemens just stood around watching the floorshow, shouting and voicifying like they was watching a boxing match, it was like a crucifixion, that's what it was like. And in all that confusion they forgot all about me, so I slipped out through the kitchen door and the darkie cooks was watching the beating too, and they was laughing their heads off, so they didn't pay no attention to me. . . .

"Lord, I tell you I ran through those streets like a ghost was after me and went to my rooming house and threw myself down on my knees and prayed the Lord for forgiveness. I ain't never seen no violence like they wreaked on Doc, and I prayed and prayed all night until the Lord told me it was time for me to go back home and beg my daddy's forgiveness, because that was the only way I could break the chain of evil I had unintentionally leashed, and that's just what I did—

"I had seventy-five dollars hid away in my suitcase and I took that money and packed my things, and when I heard Miss Hendley and the foreign gentleman come banging on the door downstairs, I just snuck out through the kitchen and started walking to the train station as fast as my feet would take me and I sat there out on the steps all night until they opened the colored ticket window the next morning and I bought me a ticket and went back home and asked my daddy's forgiveness like the Good Lord said I should, and even Preacher Gore he forgave me and explained how it had all been the devil's work to test me, but that it had served to help me learn the evil ways of the world, and I went back to singing in the church choir, and everybody said my singing was more like an angel singing than ever before, and that it was my sufferings made me sing so deep and heavenly that people would moan and fall on the floor and dance around like ghosts and generally carry on when I sang, and I knew then that I had some mysterious power in me that sometimes scared me when I thought about it, because knowing you got that kind of power over people is awesome and comes from the land where ghosts live.

"As for Doc, I don't know what happened to that poor nigger, because I never saw him again, though to tell you the honest truth, he sometimes would appear to me in dreams trying to make me give up my decision to stay a virgin all my life, and I figgered that by the way his figure was gleaming and shining so and he never said nothing, I figured he must a been dead and residing in the land of the ghosts—"

6

In her own cool detached way, Gracie was delighted with the rough draft of the notes I had assembled after my first interviews with Mona Pariss. So delighted, in fact, that—something she had never done before—she invited me to pick her up at her office on Madison Avenue and accompany her to a book party for a young, not-yet-fashionable Black poet noted for her obsession with the theme of the Pimp as Revolutionary. It was to be an anti-literary establishment affair—to distinguish it from the sterile, martini-flooded book parties of the white literary establishment—and was to be held in a homey soul food restaurant and bar on some obscure street in the Lower East Side. Frankly, I did not share Gracie's enthusiasm about the way the rough drafts of my notes were shaping up. The life of Mona Pariss, at least in this first phase of our interviews, was appearing complex, mysterious, haunting—a disturbing mosaic of almost mythical fragments, like those intricately decorated fragments of some prehistoric artifact, the form of which must first be conceived in the imagination before being deciphered and restored to its pristine reality.

Also creating an undercurrent of uneasiness in my mind as I entered the elevator to the eleventh floor where the ultra-contemporary offices of *New Black Woman Magazine* had recently been installed was the discomforting realization that I had led Gracie to believe (or at least had said nothing to contradict her self-induced fantasy) that I had to make love with Miss Pariss every time I interviewed her—and the even more discomforting sensation, not entirely paranoid, that somehow she had maliciously shared this titillating exoticism with all the women on the editorial staff—an impression that was reinforced by the suggestive gleam in the eye of the discreetly Afro-ed receptionist when I gave her my name.

Ignoring her occasional stares, I sat down on an orange leather couch to wait for Gracie (who was in a "very important editorial conference"), and started to light a cigarette before I realized there were no ashtrays around. Sheepishly I put my crumpled pack of Kent Menthols back in my pocket and began to leaf distractedly through the most recent copy of *New Black Woman Magazine* which I had already examined—mainly to try to discover what style of writing was encouraged.

I was reading for the third time a very long poem by yet another of the more fashionable young Black women poets when a door at the far end of the corridor opened and a strikingly beautiful girl appeared who instinctively I knew could be none other than Hortense Schiller, the new young food editor from Vassar with whom Gracie was in violent conflict.

Love at first sight? Perhaps—far be it from me to deny it, especially in light of my moonstruck insane behavior in the months that would follow . . .

(But first a brief aside concerning the entire subject of love at first sight. As I think I have already mentioned, one of the subjects I teach is a course in Medieval Literature which, rather than beginning with *Beowulf* as the department catalogue prescribes, I usually begin with *The Canterbury Tales*, the dirty stories of which have a stronger appeal to my working class students than the slaying of dragons, especially since many of my Brooklyn students have tribal ties with members of the Mafia. Usually, I begin with the dirty stories first, but this semester, instead of beginning with the earthier Chaucer tales, I chose that long, drawn-out medieval equivalent of the contemporary soap opera, "The Knight's Tale," a love story to end all love stories, in which the opening gimmick is the fact that two young noblemen, having been captured in a battle, were locked up together in a tower, buddies for life, friends for all eternity—until one of the young noblemen, having little else to do, happened to glance out the tiny barred window of their cell and catch a fleeting glimpse of a beautiful fair-haired maiden whom he immediately fell in love with—at first sight, as it were—while his friend for all eternity caught a fleeting glimpse of the same fair-haired maiden at approximately the same time—a difference perhaps of a fraction of second. The story continues to evolve, therefore, on who saw the fair-haired maiden first, fell in love with her at first sight, and thus had the right to call her his own lady love and dedicate to her his eternal devotion.

Does love at first sight exist? That was the subject of that day's discussion. And as a professor approaching what for the younger members of my class is middle age, I made every attempt to mask my cynicism and discuss the matter with all the psychological and sociological insight the weighty matter merited. The fact is—though I dared not admit it—that every time I have fallen in love, from earliest adolescence to more recent amatory disasters, it has *always* been love at first sight. But in the heated discussion that followed that day's discussion I could mobilize no convincing evidence to counter the snickering obstructionism of what for most of the members of the class was considered an entirely irrelevant topic—entirely unrelated, that is, to making it with a girl while munching popcorn in a drive-in movie. They looked at me as if I were some kind of a nut, a fossil nourished on William Powell and Myrna Loy films, which I was. At which point an Irish truck driver, attending college so he could become a policeman and make ten times as much money from pay-offs, his own admission, turned the class into an uproar of derisive laughter by suggesting that the two noblemen locked up in the tower were probably "queers" and that the fair-haired princess was, in reality, their jailer in drag.)

But the symptoms of my own undeniable attack of love at first sight with Hortense Schiller were all too real and familiar—the skipping heartbeat, the clamminess of the hands, the difficulty in breathing, the compulsive flaring of nostrils, the electric shock awakening of the penis (to mention only a few of those physiological reactions which I assume most men have experienced at one time or another). But there was also something else, far more mysterious and overpowering, something having to do with a strange feeling of recognition. But here words fail me. How much more eloquent was Miss Pariss when she told me of *her* moonlight encounter with Doc.

"Mr. Edwards?" Hortense Schiller said as though bestowing upon me a name rather than establishing my identity. "I'm really honored to meet you. I've read all your books. And the material you're gathering on Mona Pariss must be one of the most challenging experiences of your career—"

That subtle emphasis on "challenging" convinced me now that what I most feared had indeed happened (and, of course, I had no one to blame but myself).

"Gracie sent me out to make you comfortable—" she went on to say, having just introduced herself. "We can go to my office and chat, or stay out here if you like—"

"By all means, let's go to your office," I said.

What did she look like, since this was love at first sight? I don't know. She was beautiful, she had character, she was poised, she was taller than I was, she was very sexy the way some fifteen-year-old boys are sexy, she was wearing tight-fitting bluejeans, very expensive, and an Indian madras shirt. She had bosoms. She had kind eyes that occasionally darkened into a look of suspicion as if she were continuing a private angry conversation with herself. Her hands were expressive, and she seemed to love to smooth the contours of the sides of her hips. She was hip and homey. Her voice had a melodious Southern accent, but it was also crisp and Vassar-like when she felt like it.

She dominated the space around her by long-strided movements, but could also become soft and compliant, more as some secret spiritual discipline than as a trait of personality. She was sweet and tough. I loved everything about her, I was hooked. I estimated she was exactly twenty-one years younger than I. But, of course, I look younger than my age, though suddenly then I felt shabby, and it came as a shock to me how aged and sullen I had become, edgy and defensive, since I began this series of interviews on Mona Pariss. Especially now, as I followed Hortense Schiller down the thick carpeted hallway, past cubicles where girl employees stopped their work to mark my passing and then immediately buried their heads over an ostentatious urgency of tasks; I wished I had washed my hair, which had become thin over the forehead and must have reflected incipient baldness under the glaring fluorescent lights; I wished I had worn my brown velvet combat jacket and hounds-tooth bell-bottom trousers instead of the grey flannel suit I had retrieved out of the closet to wear on my now infrequent ventures into busy efficient mid-town glass box corporate offices—I am still terrified by the idea of being taken for an errand boy.

We entered her office and immediately my self-confidence returned. For one thing, there was no desk. Against one wall was a long carpenter table, cluttered with papers, books, an ancient typewriter, a thermos, a head of lettuce, and an iron. It was the dormitory room of a hip college student. There were two plain wicker chairs and a number of enormous pillows of perhaps Moroccan origin on the floor. She found a jar of nuts and a thermos behind a stack of books and two mugs and offered me tea. She sat cross-legged on the floor and for several minutes sat there looking at me with a quizzical smile on her face, until she sensed that I was becoming uncomfortable, at which point she suddenly smiled, completely melting my defensive expression—an expression which appears automatically on my face when my vaunted self-confidence is threatened—a certain hardening of the muscles around the mouth and a Bedouin warrior ferocity of the eyes which unfortunately intimidates no one but myself, especially my students when they become all too aware that I have entrapped myself in some sententious maze of platitudes out of which I am frantically seeking an exit.

"Not much of an office, is it?" she said teasingly from her yoga position, and she leaned on one of the huge cushions on the floor.

"I think it's delightful—I used to work in an advertising agency where the office gave me claustrophobia it was so small—"

Another silence while the muscles around my mouth hardened almost painfully. I struggled to keep my eyes roving over the room, but continually, on their own volition, they returned to the zipper of her expensive jeans.

"I've read all your books—"

This was familiar terrain, but she made no further comment, and my heart sunk to a new low.

"But I think you're really touching something basic, about the Black experience anyway, in your interview with Mona Pariss."

"They're only very rough notes. I showed them to Gracie only to prove that I was doing my job—I didn't realize she was showing them to the whole staff—"

"I xeroxed them for her—"

"Oh, I see—"

Another long silence. I forced my glance to the head of lettuce on the incredibly cluttered carpenter's table she used as a desk.

"I have rabbit blood in me," she said, following my gaze. "But really that woman's life is unbelievable—"

"Aren't most lives?"

I was regaining my customary aplomb, thank goodness—and since she insisted on sitting there at my feet like a disciple of the great literary master, the inane remark did not seem at all flippant as it spontaneously slipped out of my mouth.

"Well—you're a novelist, and a college professor too, I understand—isn't there a conflict between poetic truth and objective truth? I mean, from what I've read you find mostly poetry in this woman's life, but make no mention of the institutionalized oppression she has been exposed to as a Black Woman—"

I was pissed off, she was turning into a hyper-thyroid college radical like Melinda Rodriguez, and the nightmarish memory of that crushing humiliation that first day in my Black Lit class must have become apparent in my expression, for she smiled engagingly and said—condescendingly, I thought:

"But then those were only rough notes, poetic impressions. I'm sure you'll get around to a sound analysis of her socio-political reality when you complete your assignment—"

"You say you've read my books—?" I was determined to bring an end to this inquisition.

"Yes, I read the first one while I was in college—the last one I read when I first came to work here and they were discussing you for this particular assignment—"

"Well, did you like them?"

"I read them very carefully. You're a very gifted writer, you know. But, as with so many of our older Black writers, there is a certain self-conscious apology for being a writer—as if maybe you should bc doing something else—"

"Like what—being a pimp?"

She laughed musically and I was back in love with her.

"Are you going to the book party?" she asked. "It ought to be interesting. 'The Pimp as Revolutionary.'"

"So I've been told. It's an intriguing idea. Perverse, actually. All the revolutionaries I know wear glasses and dress like post office clerks—"

"You're talking about white revolutionaries. You've lived in Europe a long time, haven't you?"

"Well, you have to live somewhere—"

"It depends on what you call living—"

"And what do you call living?"

"Getting involved—"

"Involved in what?"

"Life—"

"Well, how can you live and not be involved in life—?"

"You'd be surprised how many living dead there are walking around—especially among Black people—"

"Are you talking about love and sex—or politics?"

She laughed again, but her laughter suddenly broke off. Without turning, I could feel that Gracie had entered the tiny office.

"I see you two have already met," Gracie said as the Ice Age set in. "Hortense is the new food editor I was telling you about—

"Hortense, baby—would you mind terribly checking out the graphics on that chitlun lay-out? The color proofs have just come in—"

"See you again," Hortense said, scrambling to her feet, smiling at me and, I think, winking. The tension between the two was electric.

"She's a very bright girl," I said.

"A smart ass—"

"Aren't all you Vassar graduates?"

"Listen—I've had a fucked-up day and I don't want any shit from you—"

"By the way, I got your check. I really appreciated it—"

"Just keep up your appointments with Miss Pariss and give me all your notes and rough drafts. In that jive editorial conference I just came out of we decided we can feature the story in at least three consecutive issues. So I'm reminding you, if you let me down on this assignment—"

"I know, I know—I think you need a drink to get yourself together—"

"They say you were looking for Hortense's ass. You're the one needs to get yourself together. Come on, let's get out of here—do you see the way she keeps this office? It's disgusting. Look at that head of lettuce. And those cushions on the floor. I'm telling you, that girl's a nut. I only hired her because her oldest sister was my roommate—"

We finally captured a taxi and headed downtown to the Lower East Side.

"Who's this poet the book party is for? I've never heard of her before."

"Name one Black woman writer you've ever heard of."

"Phillis Wheatley," I said jokingly, badly misreading her mood.

"Phillis Wheatley wrote odes to General Washington. This sister writes odes to pimps. There *is* a difference—"

"Gracie, you're in one of your evil moods—"

"And you're playing stupid games with me just because you're turned on by Hortense Schiller's infantile ass. No doubt she told you what a great writer you are while sitting at the feet of the Great Author—"

"Seriously, Gracie—you underestimate that girl. She has tremendous perceptions—"

"Of course she does. That's why I made her food editor. It takes all kinds of tremendous perceptions to figure out fifteen ways to cook yams—you know, yams with mayonnaise, yams with caviar, yams with snails and garlic—"

It was time to change the subject, but I could think of no strategic area of discussion that was not a potentially dangerous minefield. So instead I pretended to watch the traffic, which at that get-away hour was the usual panic-stricken flight from office paranoia. Gracie broke the silence, her voice warmer now and more relaxed.

"I only asked you to accompany me to this book party because you're now supposed to be one of our writers. Pure public relations for the magazine. But don't be surprised if they treat you like Uncle Remus out on a pass from the old folks home. You've lived in Europe too long, and the fact that you're an English professor—"

"Come off it, Gracie—I'm not all that new to this scene . . ."

"First of all, this isn't going to be a scene—it's going to be a race riot between Black men and Black women . . ."

The tense Puerto Rican cab driver obviously was ill at ease overhearing our conversation.

"What you say the address is?" he asked, turning his mustache toward us (and almost running down a bleary-eyed wino who was wildly cursing the occupants of an automobile who had refused him a tip for further dirtying their windshield with the filthy fragment of what looked like a stolen shroud).

Gracie efficiently pulled out her polished leather appointment book.

"Avenue A near the corner of Third Street. It's called Soul Conglomerates, Inc.—and since it's next to a police station, you shouldn't have any trouble recognizing it—"

The cab driver nodded without understanding a word of her directions, but somehow ten minutes later we pulled up in front of a drab graffiti-decorated building where a rather large crowd of young Blacks was milling about the entrance.

Gracie was immediately recognized by a committee of tough receptionists, elegantly attired male and female literary militants, and we were ushered like distinguished diplomats to the front row of the cavernous room, transformed into an improvised auditorium for the poetry reading, the debate that would follow and the inevitable autographing and book-buying ritual.

Gracie, well-known for her television appearances on "Soul" and other sundry televised debates having to do with the problems of Black women, was hugged and kissed and sistered beyond all propriety. Occasionally she would introduce me to someone as "one of her writers, the novelist, etc.," but she might as well have been introducing Stepin Fetchit at a Black Panther meeting for all the fishy-eyed looks of bewilderment I received.

On the other hand, being completely ignored, anonymous to all, except for some horn-rimmed albino Black History professor from New Jersey who mistook me for the librarian at Public School Number 73 in Newark, I was completely free as a mere spectator.

The program was late starting, but finally the lights that glared down over the gathering from the ceiling overhead (faded angels and esoteric religious patterns from the days when the edifice had been an Orthodox Greek church) dimmed and Gracie stepped up to the microphone.

There were cheers, and "go girl," and "let's hear what this heavy shit is all about" audible from the crowd, but Gracie had an air of overpowering authority and hipness about her that soon quieted down the overflowing and exuberant crowd.

"Brothers and sisters," she began, "on behalf of *New Black Woman Magazine* it is my unique pleasure to welcome here tonight one of our most controversial bad and beautiful young Black poets. Sisters, I don't have to mention her name. Anyone who doesn't know who she is and what she stands for has no business being here in the first place—"

Raucous laughter greeted this remark, and I cast a sharp glance at Gracie, paranoid again, to see if she was referring to me—but by then she had continued her introduction.

"We may not all agree with what the sister says in her poems, but *New Black Woman Magazine* believes that any time a poet has a perception as radical as the one our young guest tonight expresses in her work, you better listen or you just might miss the boat, and I'm not referring to Marcus Garvey's boat. After the reading, there will be a short question and answer period—and I mean short. So now let's give a big welcome to one of the baddest, heaviest, most scandalous, sweetest and most beautiful sisters writing the new Black poetry today—"

Given the outrageously radical theme of her poetry, the poet struck me as being as fragile and demure as an apprentice hairdresser. She had a timid smile, an almost apologetic stage presence, and was wearing an unfashionable long plaid skirt which had gone out of style at least seven years before. Her only concession to a Third World look was a loose peasant blouse of virtually transparent handmade linen through which an astonishingly erect pair of jewel-topped breasts were distractingly visible.

The drummers and a duet of flute players from the band behind her on the platform set the mood, obsessive and nostalgically lyrical, the flutists' phrasings and chord constructions attacking the consciousness almost inaudibly like radio signals from a distant planet.

Almost ten minutes passed before the poet began to read her poetry. She stood there almost motionless, as if shrinking herself into a trance-like state.

Then when the audience became so quiet and expectant that it was almost as if she were alone in the room, she began to read in a sometimes strident, sometimes crooning, sometimes Gregorian chant tone of voice.

To be truthful, I was so entranced and hypnotized by her performance, and by the rapt attentiveness of the crowded audience, that the only line I can recall, or *think* I recall, was (and I'm paraphrasing) something to the effect of "*Black woman, you been oppressed so long by the snowman master, let's melt the abominable monster, by glorifying the Pimp, gifting him with gold and diamond trappings, drape him in vestments of precious silk, let our beautiful bodies buy him spears and guns, in the degradation of our long centuries of oppression, let us transmute our oppression into the glorification of Revolution and sacred Liberation—*"

The riot began before I realized what was happening around me. It began when a hefty Welfare Rights Mother shouted "Enough of this filth! Bring our men back home so they can pay the bills and help with the dishes!"

Another voice, loud and slightly hysterical (I looked around and saw that it was the albino Black Studies Professor from New Jersey) screamed above the general shouts and catcalls that were making it by now impossible for the performance to continue: "The pimp, the pusher are the real oppressors of the youth of our

Black communities! This isn't poetry—What you are suggesting is nothing but pernicious nonsense!"

A fight broke out near the bar: two demonstrating women were struggling with a policeman who was trying to lead them away.

Two more Black policemen blew their whistles and broke through the crowd swinging their clubs. By now half the audience was standing on chairs watching the other half pushing and shoving and milling about.

From the corner where I was sitting I caught a glimpse of a fire exit and made a quick escape. I reached the street corner just as the light changed to red and hailed a taxi. Just as I was getting in, the strident yelling of the riot inside Soul Conglomerates, Inc., merging with the neighborhood noises, I heard a tremulous voice call my name:

"Mr. Edwards! Can you wait a minute!"

It was Hortense Schiller, and in a matter of seconds she was sitting next to me in the back of the cab.

"Oh, God!" she said as soon as the cab swerved recklessly into the uptown traffic. "What happened in there? It was like the assassination of Malcolm X—!"

"What happened—I think—is that the Organization of Welfare Mothers somehow heard about this Pimp as Revolutionary thing and showed up to start a riot—! Now that I think of it, wasn't there a TV camera crew parked across the street?"

"Then you think the whole thing was staged?"

"If it was, Gracie's one hell of a PR genius—"

"It was terribly unfair to the poet, disgusting—even worse, barbaric—"

Hortense moved to the far side of the back seat of the cab and seemed to be deep in thought, seemed to be waiting for me to make some preordained move. I decided this was not the time to test her opinions about writers, about the PR aspects of magazine merchandising, about The Pimp as Revolutionary. As a matter of fact, I wasn't in very much of a mood to discuss anything heavy. So I turned to her and asked:

"How about dinner?"

Hortense cheered up immediately.

"I'm starved, to tell you the truth—"

"Me too," I lied. My stomach was churning like an ice cream machine without any ingredients except rock salt.

"Where would you like to go?"

"Anywhere you say—just get me away from this depressing neighborhood—"

"How about Luchows—?" I said, naming the first restaurant that popped into my mind.

We ordered at random, neither of us wanting to pretend to know German cuisine (a plus for Hortense, I thought, for I was spared the terror of being embarrassed in front of her by one of the Hussar troopers serving as waiters). We ended up eating deer meat and potatoes and a sticky strudel washed down with a bottle of white wine as thin and tasteless as distilled battery water.

But the atmosphere was quiet and intimate and kitschy and I could pretend we were in love. But there is a kind of built-in banality to descriptions of evenings like this. There's not really very much you can say to make them sound fresh and real—so let me try to report things straight. Actually, the high point of the meal was when Hortense accidentally covered the back of my hand with a spoonful of mustard which, since we had just finished off a second bottle of wine, set us both to laughing hysterically.

We paid. The bill was over forty-seven dollars and I had to pay cash since all my credit cards had long since become overloaded. And we left the restaurant with all the Hussar troopers bowing at us as a sign of their Germanic appreciation of a budding love affair, and with the string orchestra playing angelically the love theme from some German operetta.

Outside there was a fresh breeze and the commercial streets were almost deserted. Impulsively she pulled my arm and then took me by the hand and started running up the street.

"It's a splendid night," she said, as I struggled to lower my heartbeat to keep from puffing from the exertion. "What do you say we walk up town?"

"Well—okay, why not?"

"You're not tired, are you?—I mean, after all the excitement of that wild book party?"

So we walked and walked and walked, cutting over to Fifth Avenue at 34th Street, occasionally holding hands, but mostly maintaining a brisk British army marching pace, complete with synchronized swinging arms. This extraordinary consuming of energy prevented conversation or even window shopping for that matter. But after walking through Central Park in spite of my only half-joking reference to muggers we finally decided to sit on a bench near Central Park West near 72nd Street to catch our breath and talk.

Commenting on her tremendous energy, Hortense confessed that she kept herself in shape by working out in a gym frequented by boxers. I was in such bad shape myself (although it must be admitted as a fact, not necessarily a scientific fact, that falling in love with a young girl magically summons up unsuspected dynamos of energy in an older man) that I quickly changed the subject.

Or, to be honest, I placed my hand around the back of her neck and kissed her gently on the lips. She responded. But since we were still breathing heavily from the exertion of the walk I cannot seriously claim that the kiss worked any magic.

At any rate, we went to my apartment on the 28th floor of a new building between 95th and 96th Street on Amsterdam Avenue. And quite naturally and freely we made love. While she was in the bathroom (I assumed she was inserting some contraceptive device or ingesting a pill), I chose a Vivaldi concerto and on top of that a Hugh Masekela record and on top of that a Stevie Wonder record and on top of that some obscure early seventeenth century Swedish court music as a musical background. What can I say? It was a soft lovely velveted evening, the lovemaking gentle and intimately comfortable. Hortense had just fallen asleep in my arms when the phone rang and, with that sharp infallible instinct that light sleepers and swindlers share, I knew immediately that it was Gracie.

Her voice boomed so loud over the receiver that I thought she had ordered the telephone company to turn up the volume.

"What the hell happened to you?"

"I got scared of being trampled to death."

"Why does your voice sound so skinny and mysterious? Is there someone there with you? Hortense Schiller, for example?"

"Gracie, you know damn well it's none of your business whether I have company or not—"

"That skinny-assed bitch! No doubt you had a fancy candlelight dinner, then walked uptown, stopped in the park and held hands, kissed—and then went to your apartment. That shrewd lettuce-nibbling bitch. Did she tell you what a great writer you are? That you remind her of her English teacher in high school—?"

"Gracie, are you drunk? I mean, have you been drinking? It's after two o'clock in the morning—"

"I don't give a fuck what time of the night it is, you tell that nigger she better get her skinny ass to the office on time tomorrow morning or she can start looking for a job as a welfare investigator—!"

She hung up. The Swedish court music embroidered the abrupt silence and alleviated the ringing in my ears, but was by no means an adequate antidote to the irrational sense of guilt Gracie's contrived wrath has always instilled in me. I returned to the bedroom and Hortense was still asleep, but she had changed into a fetus-like position and had moved to the opposite side of the bed.

7

About three weeks later, I met Reverend Grooms coming out of the liquor store near where the neighborhood winos hang out on the corner of Broadway and 95th Street, a few feet from the Thalia Theatre, where I was on my way to spend a quiet afternoon watching that old classic *Black Orpheus* for at least the fifth time.

He stopped in his tracks until his bleary eyes were finally able to focus on me as if undergoing a painful mental struggle in his mind as to where he had seen me before. Finally he seemed to recognize me. And, snuggling the brown bag of wine he had been carrying under his arm, he broke out into a snaggle-tooth smile and shuffled over to me with outstretched hand.

"Well, if it isn't Professor Edwards," he said, mustering an impressive stance of formal dignity. "This is indeed a pleasure. When I woke up this morning I knew this was going to be a special day. First I pick up last Thursday's paper and find out I won fifty dollars in the New York State Lottery, and now I have the unexpected honor of meeting you on Broadway . . .

"In my opinion," he continued, his dignity and self-confidence increasing as he spoke, "this calls for a celebration—and I would be greatly honored if you would join me in the bar across the street for a drink—perhaps that quiet little bar next to Nedick's—That is, if you don't mind the clientele, you being a professor and all—"

"Oh, I often go there," I lied.

It was an old Irish bar featuring cheap two-for-ninety-five-cents drinks, and reeking with the smell of vomit-soaked sawdust. We entered the dungeon-like darkness and stood at the end of the bar counter nearest the toilet.

Reverend Grooms was in a cheerful talkative mood, and all of his hostility toward me seemed to have evaporated in the euphoria of unexpectedly winning fifty dollars in the lottery.

"Yes, sir, professor," he said when the four cheap whiskies in clouded glasses were roughly shoved in front of us by the consumptive Irish barman.

"Yes, sir—this is an honor and a pleasure! To your health and success. I always admire a young man with a college education, especially when he's colored and smart like Bill Cosby—!"

"I also find Bill Cosby an extremely gifted entertainer—and an educator as well," I said, mustering a tone of sincerity and conviviality to equal that of Reverend Grooms.

"He has certainly accomplished some impressive innovations in the education of young children growing up in an age of television—" I added pompously.

"He has indeed, he has indeed—if I had half the opportunities you young folks have today—"

"Yes, I suppose things have changed a great deal since you were a young man—"

"They sure have, they sure have—most a young man could hope for in my day was to be a Pullman porter—"

"You were a Pullman porter when you were a young man?" I asked, suddenly alert, realizing for the first time that I had neglected in my interviews with Miss Pariss any reference to Reverend Grooms' relationship with her except for the time that she mentioned casually that he used to make all her costumes.

Why hadn't it occurred to me to interview him independently? Probably because I hadn't yet recovered from the terror of that nightmarish attack on the landing, when he appeared to be bent on killing me with a butcher knife.

"Oh, yes—I been a Pullman porter, I been a traveling man all my life. I only entered the ministry after my heart went bad, after I was gassed in World War I, under General Pershing's command—"

"That must have been some experience—I had no idea you'd spent time in Europe, though Miss Pariss mentioned the fact that you used to design all her costumes—"

"I designed them, but I let the women folk do the sewing—my eyes were never too good—"

"Then you've known Miss Pariss for quite a long time?"

"Professor—" he said, lowering his voice to a whisper and glancing around at the other silent drinkers in the bar as if about to release a military secret. "I'm the one discovered Miss Pariss, I'm the one designed her stage name and started her on her career—"

"When you were a Pullman porter, they didn't call you 'Doc' by any chance, did they?"

"That's what they called me—how you know that?"

"I think Miss Pariss mentioned an old friend called Doc—"

"Well, that's what they called me all right—on account of I used to wear a goatee like them German barons wore in the movies—"

"But Miss Pariss said you were killed—"

"Killed in the Great War? No, sir—I was gassed, but I wasn't killed—"

"She didn't mention your being in the war, she said you were beaten to death by some white cops in Cincinnati—"

"She tell you that? That woman can *lie*—Do I look like a ghost?"

"Not really—what I mean is, the way she described the way those cops beat you up was—"

"I ain't never been beat up by no cops! I'm a law-abiding citizen and always have been. I ain't even been bothered by the law about my drinking—And I only drink to relieve my nervous condition—"

"Then you've been with Miss Pariss all through her illustrious career?"

"That hinkty woman would still be picking peanuts down in Orlando County if it hadn't been for me discovering she could sing—"

I yelled loudly for the surly bartender to give us four more drinks, and ordered the safest most expensive scotch I could think of.

For these sudden revelations of Reverend Grooms were transforming the entire schematic outline I had worked out for Miss Pariss' life. The bartender sauntered over and glared at me as if I were trying to be some kind of wise guy and said they didn't carry any fancy brands.

"If you want to throw your money away on that quality scotch you better go over to one of those posh saloons on the East Side where the Kennedys and the Rockefellers hang out—"

"Well, four of the same—" I said quickly, pretending not to notice the snickering and winks of the derelict drunks on either side of where we were standing.

"What we been drinking is fine with me," Reverend Grooms said. "Only reason I'm drinking scotch today is because I'm celebrating winning the lottery—"

When our glasses were refilled I said, trying to keep my voice as quietly controlled as possible so that he wouldn't become belligerent thinking I was trying to catch him in a lie:

"Then you not only recognized her talent, but helped her realize her potential as well? I had no idea you were so instrumental in her fabulous international success."

"That hinkty ungrateful woman—You see how she treats me like I was some kind of army orderly and she was a general? That hinkty woman would *still* be picking peanuts down South if I hadn't come along and discovered her—"

"Well, one thing's sure—you sure aren't dead!"

"You think I'm lying, boy?" Reverend Grooms shouted.

"No, no—I'm listening. You were saying, you almost got killed in the Great War—under the command of General Pershing—"

"Miss Pariss—she don't listen to what I'm telling her either—" he said petulantly. "She don't listen to nobody but spirits and ghosts and welfare investigators—"

"Many famous artists, or entertainers, live through the ghosts and memories of the highlights of their careers—especially such a tremendously exciting and important career as Miss Pariss', on and off the stage—"

"I ain't talking about those kinds of ghosts—I've been trying for years to get that woman back to her original Christian ways before it's too late, but she don't pay me no attention, she just keeps on fooling around with all that juju mumbo jumbo—"

"Juju mumbo jumbo? You mean all those plastic saints and candles and incense burning?"

"That and worse—"

"Well, don't you think as people grow older they have a right to their private eccentricities?"

"What I'm talking about, isn't no eccentricity—that woman really believes—"

"Believes in what?"

"All that juju mumbo jumbo—what I'm talking about—"

"Surely after all her traveling all over the world—"

"Traveling ain't changed that woman one iota—down in peanut country where she come from people still believe—"

I glanced at the clock over the Miller Beer sign. Nearly an hour had passed, and Reverence Grooms was becoming increasingly incoherent, and was beginning to lose his balance. The idea of having to carry him home did not appeal to me in the least. It would spoil the mood for my evening with Hortense and would attract undue attention to me in the neighborhood, placing in jeopardy the anonymity I had come to appreciate so much living in New York. The police might even call an ambulance, and I would be trapped in the emergency room of Knickerbocker Hospital filling out reports. It was something to be avoided like the plague.

"Reverend Grooms—it's been great talking to you, but I think I have to run off to an appointment—"

"You think I'm drunk and don't know what I'm telling you about?" he snarled.

The mask of hatred and the threat of violence twisted his face into a deflated basketball and his eyes were as red as a dragon's.

I was suddenly so frightened that, for a moment, I was on the verge of just walking out. But in that moment of indecision he seized hold of my arm like a grappling hook. And held it in such a tight grip that I was afraid he might never turn it loose.

"Don't you *know* nothing, boy? You call yourself a college-educated professor—but don't you *know* nothing?"

"Sir, it's not necessary for you to yell at me—"

"But you ain't listening to me, boy—you ain't listening—"

"Listening to what?"

"What I'm trying to tell you—that woman working her juju mumbo jumbo on you!"

"Reverend Grooms, I really must go. I'll be very happy to discuss this matter with you at another time. In fact, I had planned to interview you personally about the career of Miss Mona Pariss as soon as I had accumulated the necessary basic facts of her life—"

"You better listen to me, boy. You better listen to me—"

I ordered four more of the same and when the glasses were shoved in front of us Reverend Grooms finally released his grip on my arm and I was able to leave the vile-smelling bar furtively but fast.

What was to have been a quietly pleasant afternoon at the movies had turned into a nightmare with my unexpected encounter with Reverend Grooms, so it was only to be expected that both the mood and the setting of what was to have been a pleasant evening with Hortense that evening would reflect all the malevolence of the fat old goblin's negatively charged vibes.

The moment she came in the door, her eyes red and her usually mischievous expression taut, I knew that something was wrong, something very serious.

"Gracie fired me," she said tearfully, pushing past me to pour herself a drink from my tiny bar.

"How could she do that, Lovebird?" That was the nickname I settled on as being sufficiently intimate and hip rather than the hackneyed and overworked "baby."

"She said the magazine was having financial difficulties and that they were going to have to cut down on staff, and since I was the last to be hired I'd have to be the first to be fired. She said they would handle the food editor chores as a team. But the real reason is you—"

"You mean she thinks we're lovers?"

"Well, aren't we?"

"Of course, I love you—we both know that—but I thought this was just our secret thing—"

I was lying and she knew it. In the meantime a vile smell and a dense cloud of smoke alerted me to the fact that, adding to what by now was an accumulating series of disasters, was the burning of my special spaghetti sauce.

When I returned from the kitchen Hortense was slumped in my favorite armchair. Her eyes had dried and apparently the drink had revived her spirits, for she said almost cheerfully:

"In a way I'm glad. I couldn't stand another week working with all those jive nigger would-be Gloria Steinems."

"Perhaps if I had a little talk with Gracie—"

"She wouldn't pay the slightest attention to you. She hated my guts from the day I started to work for them. She said my militant stance—her exact words—were old-fashioned 1960 sophomore attitudes. The main thing for Black people today is to reach the Black middle class through a moderate consumer-oriented media attack—Besides I think she's in love with you—"

"Gracie in love with me!" I exclaimed, pouring myself a much-needed drink and forcing a nervous laugh. "There's nothing between us, nothing but our professional relationship—"

"And a few years' sharing the same bed—"

"Lovebird, that was centuries ago—all that's a thing of the past—"

"That's not what I've heard in the ladies' room—"

"What do you mean? I mean—what are they saying about us?"

"I don't think you'd be interested. Besides, it's too weird—"

"You mean about me having to go to bed with Mona Pariss to get those interviews—?"

"Oh, I've heard that—but that's no big deal. Or is it?"

"It isn't true, you realize that, of course. It's just malicious gossip—"

"Malicious gossip or not, that's what everyone is saying—"

"Well, who gives a damn what they say? It's not true, so if you don't mind, let's forget the whole subject—"

"What are you getting so sensitive about? I'm the one who just lost my job. I came here for love and understanding—"

Her laugh was ominous and disconcerting.

"You can have both, I promise—if you tell me what they're saying about me and Gracie—"

She paused and gazed mischievously into her glass as if to calculate the effect her words would have on me.

"They're saying that one of the reasons I'm losing my job is to take my measly salary off the accountant's books so she can pay you all that money you're getting for the Mona Pariss series—"

"You've got to be kidding! Why, I've never heard anything so ridiculous in my life. I'm being paid peanuts for those articles, and I'm even getting those goober nuts in dribbles. I'm telling you that assignment is nothing but one big headache—"

"Then why don't you come to Africa with me this summer when school's out?"

"Africa? Why Africa?"

"You know that uncle of mine in Atlanta? The rich one with the real estate and insurance rackets? Well, he and some other fat Black cats have set up a tax-free foundation to give financial support to the various African liberation movements. He's arranged for me to go as some kind of coordinator or something—Anyway, I'll be going sometime late in June—"

"Black businessmen helping African liberation movements—I don't believe it."

"Lovebird, your generation gap is beginning to show beneath your thinning hair. Don't you know *anything* about what's going on among Black people in this country since the prehistoric days of the Panthers and Poor People's Marches?"

"Well, if that book party and all that nuttiness about The Pimp as Revolutionary is any indication, I don't think I want to know—"

"You know damn well Gracie set up that whole show, Welfare Mothers included, as a media stunt to publicize the magazine—"

I put a Stevie Wonder series of records on the hi-fi, set the table, and we ate veal chops with lemon slices and salad and drank a couple of bottles of Lambrusco. No spaghetti.

Afterwards, Hortense cleared the table, dumping everything in the sink, and then we settled down to watch the Late News before going to bed.

"What are you thinking about?" she asked finally when I switched off the news, then turned down the sound.

"Going to Africa," I lied. "I've never been to Africa, it sounds like a wonderful idea. But where will I get the money?"

"Isn't Gracie paying you a fortune for the Mona Pariss series?"

"I told you I was getting peanuts. Besides I've already spent practically all of the measly advance—"

"What about doing a series for *Ebony*?"

"No chance—"

"Well, don't worry about the money. My uncle's filthy rich, owning a day care center, a private hospital, a Leisure Hospitality Home for Senior Citizens, and several funeral parlors, besides the insurance company and being on the Board of Directors of a number of banks, including a white cracker backed country agricultural bank—and making big contributions to both the Democrats and Republicans."

"Lovebird," I said, "I love you—but I couldn't take your money for something like that. Maybe I can get a loan from the professional staff credit union—"

"You know damn well I'm a rich nigger bitch, so take advantage of it while you can. In the meantime, what do you say we go to bed? That Late Show always makes me feel horny—"

"And just think," she added as she revealed her magnificent nakedness in the glow from the security lights on the corner of the terrace. "I don't have to go to work tomorrow. I can just lay here in bed and watch all the idiot give-away shows until you get back from school—"

8

The question was raised by a tall Black girl in the back row who, from the papers she had turned in, had a remarkable questioning mind.

We had finished our reading and discussion of Richard Wright's *Native Son* and were continuing a final discussion in preparation for the essay examination I usually require at the completion of each book that is read in the Black Lit class.

She was a quiet thoughtful girl from Brooklyn who wore her hair in the currently fashionable "corn-row" style. Timidly, tentatively, she raised her hand, and when finally she caught my attention, she asked in a barely audible voice:

"Professor Edwards, why are our Black authors—or at least the ones I've read so far—so negative. For example, how come they're always talking about Black people as though they're some kind of sociological disease. Take Bigger Thomas—I don't find him typical at all. He was just one dumb street nigger whose dumb actions naturally led to his dumb downfall—"

"I think you miss the point," I said, secretly agreeing with her, but for different reasons.

"As I've said many times, Bigger Thomas was meant by Richard Wright to represent a certain type of symbolic contemporary situation—the rootless, alienated derelict floating contemporary man, not necessarily Black since his type is to be found in most highly industrialized societies, giving rise to Fascism and Nazism, who is the urbanized refuse, the garbage, thrown out and abandoned by a ruthless profit-oriented economy where the Bigger Thomases all over the world have become all too frequently the metaphor for contemporary man in general—even the affluent white middle classes. At least I think that was what Richard Wright was trying to say. Writers often begin with a thesis, even a political sociological thesis as in the case of Richard Wright's *Native Son*—but other more poetic influences and intuitions often take over, and I suppose that is why literature is so fascinating—"

The girl frowned. I knew that I had not answered her question and that my phrasing was, to say the least, pompous. I sat behind my desk tapping a ballpoint pen on the attendance record book waiting for her to continue the question that really was on her mind.

"Well, Professor Edwards," she said finally, glancing around at her Black nursing student girl friends seated on either side of her in the back row, all of whom were secretly smiling as though this was a subject they had discussed amongst themselves before. "You're a writer, I mean you write books. I've never read any of them—"

"I won't hold that against you as long as you read the books assigned in class—"

There was a rustling of suppressed laughter which the girl ignored, then, impetuously, she asked:

"Why don't Black writers ever write about real people—Why do they always treat Black people like social problems—for example, of all the books you've assigned us this semester there isn't even one of them a love story. I'm sure you don't mean to imply that when Bigger Thomas smothers that white girl to death and then tries to stuff her in the furnace he is doing that out of a feeling of love—"

"In that particular incident in the novel I think what Richard Wright is trying to symbolize is the psychological Pavlovian reaction to fear that derives from psychological entrapment. Remember the rat trapped in the corner in the opening incident?"

"I understand all that, I mean I understand the psychological and sociological thesis, but Black people are tired of being studied under a microscope like they're some kind of social disease. Why don't Black writers write about love, for example?"

At that Melinda Rodriguez snorted with laughter.

"Who has time for love when you're always being oppressed? Anyway love is nothing but a bourgeois fantasy trip—"

"There have been love stories written by Black writers," I said, "for example—"

But Melinda Rodriguez' mocking expression created a total blank in my mind. Instead I said:

"I am sure there will be some most beautiful Black love stories in the future—"

"Written by you, Professor—?"

Whatever my instinctive antagonism to Melinda Rodriguez' doctrinaire politics, I had to admit she was well-informed and sharp.

On the other hand, the unexpected direction the class discussion was taking was making me feel uneasy, and for all too obvious reasons. But after a moment of panic I decided there was no possible way that anyone in the class, especially that silent chorus of nursing students in the back row, could know anything about my private life—one of the major advantages of teaching in an urban commuting college.

So I relaxed, stared thoughtfully out of the window as Dr. Phillips my absent-minded sexless philosophy teacher used to do when I was in college, folded my hands behind my neck, leaned back in my chair and said:

"Perhaps this whole concept of romantic love is essentially a Western European concept, that derives from the Middle Ages—courtly love, the Madonna cult, the feudal system—that sort of thing. Perhaps love for Black people means something else, less fantasy, less individualism, less a property-oriented sense of exclusion possession—"

"Well, I'll buy that—" Melinda Rodriguez broke in. "All this love bullshit is a capitalist invention to sell products and exploit cheap labor—!"

"Well, let's take a quick run-down on the history of love in Western societies and maybe that way we'll come up with an answer to your question—" I looked at my watch, saw there were about twelve minutes left to the class hour, purged all thoughts of Hortense Schiller from my mind, ignored the restless shuffling of feet and the groans of boredom, and began what was to have been a quick and concise history of love in Western Society, and why Black writers do not find love a particularly congenial theme to write about—even though the juke boxes and pop singers moan about nothing else but "Baby, Baby—I love that man of mine, why you treat me so bad, etc., etc."

"But first let me put a question to the class that I asked another class when we were discussing a story dealing with romantic love—Is there such a thing as 'love at first sight'?"

"Professor Edwards, what kind of jive's this you layin' down?" Baby Blue Hawkins, the tall star basketball player, and boss campus grass dealer, said impatiently, gathering up his books and preparing to leave the classroom, as indeed everyone else in the room was except the coterie of nursing students in the back row.

"I thought this class was about Black writers of the twentieth century, heavy cats like Malcolm X, Cleaver, Stokely, heavy cats like that—and here you are running down some jive about romantic love and the Middle Ages. Shit! On my block if a dude digs a chick he does a buck and wing, makes a comment on what nice upholstery she got, and if she digs him and he digs her, that's it—"

The bell rang and I realized I had lost yet another round with my Black Lit class, and the raucous laughter that exploded like the sudden electric crackling of a summer storm made me wish I had one of those enormous beach umbrellas to hide under.

9

I was sitting in my office just about to open a virgin copy of Richard Wright's account of his first trip to Africa, *Black Power*, which I had just withdrawn from the college library, when Miss McCoy, the department secretary, announced coyly that I had a phone call, a woman, and that, if I wanted to, I could take the call on the extension line at the far end of the room where "I would have more privacy."

I don't get many calls at the college, and I was certain it was a bill collector, but instead Gracie's booming voice thundered through the receiver:

"What's all this bullshit about you running off to Africa with that slut Hortense Schiller?"

Gracie's voice was coming across so loudly that I curved the palm of my hand over the receiver and stole a glance at Miss McCoy who, though pretending to be running off someone's quiz on the ditto machine, was half-leaning in the direction of the phone, finely tuning her sensitive radar ears to pick up the signals of what had all the promise of an incipient campus scandal.

"I can hear you, you don't have to yell!"

"I'm not yelling, I'm just telling you—that screwball slut of yours is going around telling everyone in the office you and she are going off to Africa together!"

"There is no reason for you to insult the girl—after firing her the way you did. The last to be hired, the first to be fired! What's she doing in the office anyway?"

"She came to pick up her head of lettuce and the rest of her sophomoric garbage—and to spread the word that you two were running off to Africa together on some kind of safari honeymoon!"

By now Miss McCoy was frantically turning the handle of the ditto machine while shamelessly listening even though the sheets of paper flowing from the machine were falling all over the floor like snow leaflets.

"Listen, I don't know what you see in that bitch—but that's your business. Anybody who will go to bed with an eighty-four-year-old woman is capable of anything. But you get one thing straight—that Mona Pariss series better be ready for the copy department no later than March 15th to make the publishing deadline. We've already announced the series, and our business manager doesn't play when it comes to deadlines! You fuck up on this and I'll put a contract out on your ass!"

"Gracie, I have only one or two more interviews, the other tapes are being typed. I'm writing day and night on the story—"

"With Hortense Schiller's panting breath blowing inspiration in your ears—"

"You've been unfair to that girl from the beginning. She told me all about how you wouldn't give her the key to the executive ladies' room until she complained to her older sister—the one that was your roommate at Vassar—"

"There was nothing personal about that, it was only staff policy. She's not only a bitch, she's a jive two-timing lying nigger bitch—"

"Where are you calling from? After all, this is an institution of higher learning and your yelling can be heard all over the English Department. Can't you talk in civilized tones for a change?"

"I don't give a shit about your crummy English Department. I want you to finish that series on Mona Pariss, fast, or there's going to be a memorial service for another talented Black artist at the Pleasant Funeral Parlor—with Ossie Davis presiding!"

There was a long pause, obviously someone had entered Gracie's office. Miss McCoy had already run off to the ladies' room to divulgate and elaborate on whatever it was she heard—which must have been plenty.

But suddenly Gracie's voice came over the receiver again, childish and plaintive:

"Baby, don't let that girl run over you like that. You deserve someone better. You've got talent, intelligence—you've got a lot to offer—"

"Hortense Schiller is not running over me," I retorted indignantly, my voice rising. "She's being sent to Africa on an important mission which, unfortunately, I am not at liberty to speak about at this time. She invited me to go with her and I agreed, when the Spring term is over. It's as simple as that. As far as the Mona Pariss interviews are concerned I've gathered reams of material. Why just the other day I interviewed Reverend Grooms, the man who claims he not only discovered her but has been her constant companion ever since. When you read the material you'll see it's pure dynamite—"

Her voice seemed almost tearful, tiny and Shirley Templish. I felt like a shoddy fraud.

"Baby, Baby darling—please don't let me down!"

10

Lying there side by side in the subdued funeral parlor lighting of her temple-like bedroom, Mona Pariss was strangely silent that evening as she thoughtfully took bird-bath-like sips from her third glass of scotch.

Frowning in the semi-darkness, turning and twisting on the enormous bed, I was debating with myself whether or not this was the proper time to mention my conversation with Reverend Grooms.

But then Miss Pariss spoke and her voice seemed to steal forth like a mist blown in from a long distance at sea:

"Like I said, they treated me royally everywhere I sang. I don't mean I was no toast of Paris like Josephine Baker, because I didn't sing that kind of dippin' and doodlin' music. I mean, I never made no monkey out of myself just to please some highfalootin' audience of dukes and duchesses. I just sang my simple songs from down home, and people respected me for it. Lot of them royalty people never heard down home church music before, all they ever heard was darkie ragtime carrying on, and I tell you those European audiences, some of them would have tears in their eyes when they would stand up clapping and yelling for more.

"Few minutes ago you ask me if I was happy and proud of all that success. Well, to tell you the truth, all my life I been one of those people got sadness tattooed all over their heart. Course, I liked those fancy hotels, and I loved going to fancy restaurants, and I was always being invited to castles and mansions with waiters in tuxedoes standing so close behind me I could hardly enjoy my food . . .

"But all that fancy living, it didn't take away the sadness that was lying there asleep inside me like a ghost just waiting there to wake up. Even then, after all those years I'd still wake up in the middle of the night from dreaming that Doc was standing at the foot of the bed all dressed in white in his heavenly glow, beckoning for me.

"Didn't scare me, mind you, but I knew it *signified* a message from the other world, and more than anything else, it kept me from getting carried away with all that darkie hoopla that was going on in Europe after the Big War when there weren't enough darkies to go around to keep people doing all that flapper dancing and frittling away their religious heritage as if the world had been saved and the new age of eternal life had begun."

"You must have been making a lot of money," I said cautiously.

"Money never meant much to me except it helped speed up the days and keep you from thinking too much about morbid thoughts all the time. Mostly my manager managed all the money and invested it in stocks. That same foreign man, the one Miss Hendley introduced me to in that rooming house in Cincinnati where all the Pullman porters used to hang out, when they beat up Doc and killed him to death . . .

"Course, when the stock market crashed, I didn't have a penny to my name and that was the last I heard of him. Later on I heard he killed himself, jumped out of a window like a lot of white folks was doing in those first depression days. . . ."

"You said that Reverend Grooms used to make all your clothes or costumes for you.—"

"I didn't say he *made* them, he *designed* them. In those days Reverend Grooms was a decent attentive colored gentleman, kind of light-skinned and suave, and if he would've been born in President Kennedy's time, they would have made him an ambassador to some African country, that was the kind of man he was. I remember once—we was touring Edinburgh, that's in Scotland—and some young aristocratic gentlemen with canes and top hats and all came into my dressing room without knocking while Reverend Grooms was tying up my corset. And you should have seen how diplomatic he was with them. Why, he shamed those white aristocratic gentlemen to death. They apologized, bowed, and left—and the next morning a big box with three dozen roses was brought to my hotel room with a long apology written on a card, and the card had royal crests. I still got that card somewhere in my trunk, but I guess they threw my trunk away with most of my mementos from those days when I couldn't pay the storage anymore after I had to go on welfare. . . ."

It was at this point that I was sorely tempted to mention the discussion I had had with Reverend Grooms in the bar, but instead I said:

"You and Reverend Grooms must have been friends a very long time—"

She laughed, strangely I thought—but it might only have been my heightened imagination.

"Me and that old wino been friends a long time, a *long long* time—"

"He goes by the name of Reverend Grooms—is he an ordained minister?"

"He took a correspondence course in some mail-order Divinity School—and during the Depression years we had a church down in Decatur, Georgia, together, and then we opened one in Harlem—but his drinking led to his downfall, though he still has the spiritual strain in his blood, if he'd only control his drinking habits—"

"And when you were stranded in Europe when the Depression broke out, then what did you do—?"

"I forgot how we got back, but we got back. All I remember was we traveled on an old luxury liner that was carrying freight and going out of service and that we paid our way by Reverend Grooms serving as the Captain's waiter, and I slept in what used to be the first-class ladies' room and did some cleaning and kitchen work. But we got back, and to tell you the honest truth, I was glad to get back to the good old U.S.A.—"

"But those were the Depression years—"

"Those Depression years didn't surprise colored folks hardly at all. Black people been living in a depression ever since Emancipation Day—and you notice Emancipation Day ain't no American holiday for Black *or* white. They got Mother's Day, Father's Day, Memorial Day, down in Orlando County when I was growing up they even had National Peanut Day—"

"But how did you live—?"

"Well, Reverend Grooms, of course, being a reverend and all could always pick up a little change with his preaching. I worked as a maid on the East Side, right smack on Fifth Avenue because of my European polish. Then one day I was serving a party on my day off, and who do I run into but my old manager's son, and he got me this job singing in a speakeasy. That's when I started singing blues and jazz kind of songs and started making what they used to call race records. I didn't make much money, as a matter of fact, I kept my job with the rich folks mostly on account of I had got used to eating fancy food in Europe, and the work was light because they didn't have any kids and they was so fussy and clean I could do that penthouse apartment in fifteen minutes if I set my mind to it. They even gave me a key so I could get in when I got back from my nightclub engagements—"

"Miss Pariss, I ran into Reverend Grooms the other day on Broadway. We had a few drinks together—"

"That was nice. He don't usually frequent no bars, that must've been the day he found out he won the New York State Lottery—"

"As a matter of fact, he did mention winning fifty dollars—"

"I suppose he told you a lot of lies. When that man drinks hard liquor, his personality changes just like Frankenstein. As long as he sticks to red Gallo wine, he's fairly decent and manageable. But as soon as he gets hard liquor in him—"

"Oh, he was very sociable, very sociable. He apparently is a great admirer of yours—"

"Yes, child, that old wino and me we been through hell and high water and back and we still fight a lot. For example, I don't like the way he lacks respect when he visits *my* house for *The Bill Cosby Show*, and only once in a blue moon will he ever invite me over to *his* apartment to cook and serve me a dinner of ham hocks and potato salad—But I tell you something, youngblood—

when you get to be up in the years like me, you appreciate *any* friend, and you get used to their ways like you gets used to a stinking tennis shoe—if you pardon the reference—"

"Another thing he was telling me about was when he used to work as a Pullman porter as a young man—"

"He tell you that? That man would tell his own mother he was suckled by a she-wolf. Don't you believe anything that old wino says—not if you want to write down the true facts of my life and career. Don't you pay a word of attention to what that man says or what you write won't be worth printing on toilet paper—"

Her eyes were drooping and she was falling asleep, so for nearly twenty minutes I just remained still and quiet until her breathing became soft and regular.

11

It was late in May and the semester was rapidly drawing to a close. And, though late in arriving, midst hailstones and thunderstorms, spring had come to New York—a startling festival of bright sunlight reflected on glass, and budding green on winter sordid streets.

One morning, while Hortense was still in bed, and I was gathering my papers together in my briefcase to drive off for school, a special delivery letter arrived. The handwriting was barely legible and my name, simple as it is, was misspelled—*Edwerds* instead of *Edwards*. There was no return address on the long envelope which was of the type used for wedding announcements or funerals. It was from Reverend Grooms and in a sprawling lopsided half-printed and half-fancy baroque script it invited me to have dinner at his apartment the following night, no later than eight p.m. please.

As a matter of course, I took Hortense along. By now she was actively helping me with the preparation of the Mona Pariss interviews, and was extremely helpful in typing up the transcripts of the conversations, and even proved unexpectedly competent in editing the language which I would promptly deliver to Gracie to reassure her that I was hard at work on the assignment.

There had been an English Department meeting dealing with the always touchy issue of promotions which left me in a slightly depressed mood, and a four-car accident on the West Side Highway kept traffic at a snail's pace. It was quarter to eight when I arrived home. There was time for a quick shower and a strong drink of scotch, several of which Hortense had already partaken of—as she put it "to get myself together in case something had happened to you."

"But what *could* have happened to me, darling?" I said, as she snuggled up against my naked body while I was maneuvering dull razor blade over my chin.

At eight o'clock sharp we were knocking at Reverend Grooms' door. The doorbell, of course, was out of order, and apparently he had been standing at the door peering out of the peephole, for the door opened immediately, without the usual screeching of locks and unravelling of chains.

After a furtive vindictive glance across the landing toward Mona Pariss' door, he invited us inside.

Whether or not it was my imagination, I cannot say, but Reverend Grooms seemed younger, certainly not a wino bum, and he introduced us into his apartment with all the elegance and aloof courtliness of a Pullman porter inviting a Southern senator into the executive parlor car of the old *Washington Limited.*

Indeed, the interior of his apartment was as unlike Mona Pariss' temple of memory and meditation, with its cluttered mementos, plastic saints, and pink boudoir lighting, as a funeral parlor is from a catering establishment. It was small, narrow, and there was only one window which had no curtain, but was covered with a single green shade, which apparently had never been raised, since the edges were tacked to the window sill.

The apartment was spare of furniture. There were three small tables of the size and shape of tables in a dining car, each with four faded plush seats, all lined up on one side of the wall. In the center of the room there was a long narrow faded red carpet of the type that also might have been part of the furnishings of a dining car. On the other side of the room were three short church pews, though they were not placed in a row facing either a real or imaginary pulpit, but were set side by side so that they formed a rather attractive divan arrangement.

The walls were all painted a gleaming white, and though there were some visible cracks in the plaster, the apartment, on first view, was as immaculate as an East Side psychiatrist's waiting room.

There were no paintings or cheap wall decorations. But there was a framed collection of old railroad calendars, all featuring those charging symbols of American progress and economic invincibility, gleaming black locomotives, painted with photographic realism to denote speed and power. Under each lithograph was the name of the train, all of them legendary in their day—there was even a huge framed reproduction of the *Royal Scot,* which I remember seeing and visiting as a babe-in-arms when it passed through Pittsburgh on an American tour.

In short, the interior of Reverend Grooms' apartment was an approximate duplication of the interior of an old-fashioned dining car, and the illusion of youth and erectness (an illusion which contrasted so sharply with his pathetic blathering drunkenness the last time we had met in that squalid stinking Irish bar on Broadway) which I now appraised in him was due to the fact that he was wearing a different, well-tailored suit—the hard finish, if slightly frayed, brass-buttoned uniform of a dining car head waiter.

And it was with the professional dignified casualness of a dining car headwaiter that he led us to the pews, then slightly bowed his head as Haile Selassie might make some barely perceptible signal to his courtiers, that it would be quite all right now if his honored guests were to take seats and partake of the hospitality of his house.

There being three pews lined up against the immaculate white plastered wall, we each sat with solitary dignity in one of them. Hortense to the right, the Reverend Grooms in the middle, and I on the pew nearest the door. From the kitchen came the pleasant odor of meat cooking.

For several moments, perhaps, awed by the unexpected austerity and dignity of the surroundings, we sat stiffly in silence. I, especially, was in a mood of expectant astonishment, even solemnity, and could think of nothing to say. Then, when the silence became almost palpable, Reverend Grooms turned to me and said in a tone of voice that was almost intimidating in its quiet tone of reproach:

"You haven't yet interrogated *me* in respect to the details of the career of Miss Mona Pariss as you said you would—"

I thought a moment before replying. Then to gain time, I said: "I was waiting for my research assistant—"

And I pointed to Hortense sitting primly and erect in her pew.

"I was waiting for Miss Schiller, here, to assist me—until recently her duties at *New Black Woman Magazine* prevented her from assisting me in the main body of research—"

"I see—I see," Reverend Grooms said, folding his hands piously over his protruding stomach. "Yes, I can understand that—and, if I may add, she is indeed a very charming young lady to be your assistant—*young and beautiful*—"

Obviously referring to what he fancied was my relationship with Miss Pariss, and barely able to restrain his relief that I was distracted romantically by Hortense, he regained his momentarily obscured suaveness and ceremoniously offered us each a drink—good scotch, Miss Pariss' brand.

We sipped our drinks in silence while Reverend Grooms trafficked in the kitchen preparing dinner. He appeared only once in the doorway of the kitchen to remark:

"Fine quality pork is *so* difficult to procure these inflationary times. I do hope the dinner will prove satisfactory to you—"

We had finished our drinks and were exchanging glances, wondering whether he intended to offer us a second drink before dinner, when he again appeared in the kitchen doorway—this time carrying a huge tray, waiter fashion, with covered chafing dishes.

He placed the tray on a side table, and from the kitchen he brought two linen tablecloths bearing the motto of some ancient railroad, the name of which I had never heard. Then he set the table meticulously, with plates bearing the same monogram and the fancy scrolled letters: *Southern Limited*. Then there was the silver with the same monogram—heavy silver with all the proper forks and knives set in the Continental fashion.

Were we to have a five-course dinner? I wondered.

No. The meal consisted of pork chops and homefried potatoes and a store-bought pumpkin pie with sprayed whipped cream decorating each slice in a star pattern.

While we ate at the first table, he stood over us and served, slightly intimidating us as though a butler were standing over us observing critically and somewhat disapprovingly our table manners. So we ate the pork chops and homefries and fancily decorated store-bought pumpkin pie in silence—though, in truth, to interrupt what was becoming an ordeal, I said timidly:

"Aren't you having dinner, Reverend?"

He said nothing, ignoring the question as though it were unworthy even of consideration.

I tried again:

"You mentioned, sir, in your invitation that you might have some interesting additional information to give us in our research into the life of Miss Mona Pariss—"

"Later, later—" he said cryptically.

Then he sat down at the last table upon which the tray and chafing dish were resting and in less than five minutes wolfed down the remains of the pork chops and homefries, alternating a bite of pork chops with a bite of pumpkin pie and finishing off the remains in a kind of frenzied dumping of all the remains of the plates into one.

Then he carefully wiped his mouth and greasy face with one of the monogrammed napkins, rose once again to his butler stance next to our table. And he bent over, like a smart lawyer whispering secret advice into the ear of a credulous client, and said so that only I could hear:

"What I am going to divulge to you, please keep to yourself—Miss Pariss must know nothing of what I am about to tell you. . . ."

And with that he began skillfully, professionally, clearing the table as though he had to rush the customers out for a second sitting.

Hortense offered to help. She even rose from her seat, but quickly sat down again when he fixed her with a frown and evil disapproving stare.

"You are my guests—please sit down."

When next he appeared from the kitchen he brought two tiny brandy glasses which he offered us with courtly gestures. He offered me a cheap cigar which I dared not refuse though the mere odor of cigars is enough to make me vomit.

When he saw that we were comfortably relaxed in our pews, he again retired to the kitchen. This time he stayed nearly twenty minutes, and there was no sound of movement.

The glances Hortense and I exchanged this time were openly afraid. But he finally came back into the room, an air of triumph on his now flushed face.

"Forgive me for neglecting you, my guests, for such a long time. But with age, my eyesight has recently declined, and I had some difficulty finding that which I am about to deliver unto you in sacred trust—"

When he finally negotiated his considerable bulk onto the undersized chair, he sat there in silence for a few minutes puffing and wheezing (the wheezing consoles in his chest even more audible in that by now oppressive silence).

Then from the top pocket of his suit he pulled out a faded postcard with a faded photograph of a younger Miss Pariss on it.

He handed me the card, and as I examined the photograph without comment, he told me to turn the postcard over. On the back of the postcard there was an address:

"Halbrin Theatrical Storage Company, Straight Street, Brooklyn, New York. . . ."

Another long dramatic pause during which I passed the faded postcard to Hortense to examine. Then Reverend Grooms said in a strange strident, almost menacing, tone of voice:

"There is where that ungrateful woman keeps her trunk—go to that establishment, and you will find all you need to know of the life of Mona Pariss—all that remains of her riches and talent!"

Abruptly then he pulled himself up from the chair and stood unsteadily in front of us. Apparently he had been drinking enormous quantities of red Gallo wine during his prolonged absences in the kitchen. And there was no longer any pretense of regal elegance or headwaiter suaveness as he said:

"You may leave now—both of you—and it is in the best interest of all of us here present that we never meet again!"

My last image of Reverend Grooms was of a pair of malevolent red eyes peering out through the crack in his door as both Hortense and I started to run down the dark stairs.

12

There was no Halbrin Theatrical Storage Company listed in the Yellow Pages of the telephone book we anxiously leafed through the moment we returned to my apartment.

We checked and rechecked the barely legible address on the back of the faded photograph of a younger Miss Pariss on the reverse side.

Finally, it was time for the Late News, and watching the shadowy rehash of the day's events, we drank ourselves into a sleepy stupor to recover from that odd mysterious visit with Reverend Grooms and went to bed.

The next day, being Saturday, we got into Hortense's battered Volkswagen and drove to the Bay Ridge section of Brooklyn where finally we located a blind alley bearing the name of Straight Street.

There we found a crumbling red brick building which looked as if it might once have been a warehouse, but which now was a mere shell serving as a parking lot for trailer trucks, most of them unmarked.

At first it appeared that there was no one around. Then a fat watchman wearing an ill-fitting watchman's uniform and carrying a prominent gun on his brass-studded belt appeared from behind the cab of one of the trailer trucks where apparently he had been relieving himself, for he was still buttoning up his trousers as he approached us, a menacing grimace on his unshaven southern Italian face.

"What are you two doing hanging around here?"

"We are trying to locate a warehouse that used to be called the Halbrin Theatrical Warehouse, and this is the closest to the address that was given us we could find. . . ."

Intimidated by the man's gun and his narrowed suspicious roving eyes, I handed him the faded postcard and address.

"You got to be kidding," he said, examining first the faded photograph and then the address. "This postcard is dated way back in the nineteen thirties—what are you, some kind of narco wiseguy?"

I assured the watchman that we were truly interested in finding the old warehouse, and when I slipped him a ten-dollar bill which Hortense had surreptitiously handed me while the watchman again began examining the faded postcard, his expression softened somewhat.

"I tell you what," he said, leading the way to the corner of the narrow pot-holed street where Hortense's Volkswagen was parked.

"You see, down here at the docks, we got to be careful with outsiders. No offense meant," he added quickly, "we got plenty of colored guys driving trucks around here. But this here address is where that theatrical warehouse *used* to be, and there's only one guy I can think of would know where maybe they're located at the present. So why don't you two sit in your car and have a smoke while I make a couple of telephone calls around."

He was gone for nearly forty minutes by my watch and when he returned he was shaking his head with dramatic pessimism.

"The Halbrin still exist—but it's been taken over by a bunch of Puerto Rican middlemen, and it's now located somewhere way up in the Bronx. My connection didn't know the exact address, but he did give me the name of the Puerto Rican fellow. He might know where it is. You got a pencil and a piece of paper?"

I pulled out my address book and Hortense gave me a ball-point pen and we copied as best we could the watchman's bizarre handwriting.

Then as we started up the motor, anxious to get away from the slightly sinister Bay Ridge dock area, which on that Saturday morning seemed even more ominous than at night because of its being nearly completely deserted, the watchman stuck his head through the window and winked, or at least I thought he winked—it might have been some kind of nervous tick.

"You sure you ain't some kind of narcos?" he asked again in that gravel Bay Ridge voice of his.

"You can be sure we are only interested in locating the trunk of a once famous entertainer," Hortense said, bestowing on the watchman her most endearing innocent smile.

"Oh, you two in showbiz? I got a daughter got an audition coming up next week with the Lawrence Welk show—"

By then Hortense had shoved the battered car in gear and we were careening around the corner, barely colliding with a speeding truck pulling into the parking lot from a side street.

The watchman was waving and examining the ten-dollar bill and his thick wet lips seemed to be saying:

"Good luck, you'll need it—"

The slow tortuous route to the Bronx led us through Harlem, past the Afro wig stands on 125th Street, and across the Bronx Expressway to a desolate area of enormous clustered highrise housing projects.

For some reason, probably having to do with the esoterics of real estate speculation, or the refusal of some stubborn heir to die, the Halbrin Theatrical Supply Warehouse was located right in the very center of the housing project, fenced in by a wire fence, with an access road that led through the community housing project playground and past a statue to the first Negro mess boy killed in World War II.

This time we had little difficulty in locating the office of the warehouse, because a battalion of Black and Puerto Rican youths were working, chain-gang fashion (the summer city employment program) unloading two truckloads of watermelons for the housing project association's annual picnic.

"Yes, this is the office of the Halbrin Theatrical Warehouse," a mustached smiling Puerto Rican guard in rolled-up shirt sleeves and green- and purple-striped platform shoes said in answer to our question as he continued leafing through a Spanish-language photo romance magazine while occasionally supervising the unloading of the watermelons through a heavily barred window beside the door to his office.

"What can I do for you?"

"We are trying to locate a trunk placed in storage a number of years ago when the warehouse was located in Brooklyn—"

"Oh, yes—with our Italian friends—"

"That's right, in Bay Ridge—the Halbrin Theatrical Storage Warehouse—"

"I heard you the first time—we are under new management now, but here we keep everything, everything—"

He casually cast aside his sex magazine and pulled out a crooked cigar which he lit meticulously and filled the narrow office space with the very type of acrid cigar smoke that causes me to vomit.

But I fought back the automatic stomach contractions and, taking advantage of the leering glances of appreciation that he was casting in the direction of Hortense's magnificently rounded derriere, I ventured:

"We have the name and the date—"

"My friend, you are fortunate we are open today—because we are unloading the watermelons for the project festival—let me see the name and address please—"

Hortense handed him the faded postcard and cast a look of pessimism in my direction. The watchman, however, seemed to find nothing unusual either in the faded postcard or even the date.

"Ah, but this has been in storage quite some time, I wasn't even born yet in 1932. Though I look rather old for my age, I am really only twenty-seven. You see, I believe in enjoying life—"

And he threw back his melon-shaped head and laughed.

"Nineteen thirty-two," he said finally after he caught his breath. "How many years is that? My American arithmetic ain't too good—"

"Forty years minus a few months—" Hortense replied with the rapidity of an electronic calculator.

"A half century—one half of one hundred years—"

He scratched his greased hair in wonder and perhaps puzzlement until finally a sly look of cupidity crept into his narrowed eyes, though his smile grew wider, revealing a magnificent set of rapacious teeth.

Obviously money was on his mind.

"One half of one hundred years, that is a long time for a trunk to be in storage. What is in it—the bones of a saint?"

He laughed heartily again and then broke off abruptly.

"Once we got a request for an old trunk like this—and do you know what was inside?"

He paused suspensefully for maximum dramatic effect and then said:

"Nothing—it was absolutely empty—there was nothing in the trunk. You should have seen the expression on those greedy faces. They must have been relatives or something and thought it was filled with gold!"

"I know this is Saturday and that you are extremely busy unloading watermelons for the project festival—but could you give us an idea how much it would cost to get the trunk, or even if you can locate it for us—"

"Locate it for you, of course we can locate it for you. The Halbrin Theatrical Workshop has a reputation for not throwing anything away—*not anything*!"

But now he waddled close in front of us, the smell of garlic competing with the strong odor of urine rising from the open door of the yellow-stained toilet.

"But there is, of course, the matter of the fee—money—"

(And he scraped thumb and finger together to ignite our thoughts in the righteous direction of financial considerations.)

"But today is Saturday," he said in a conspiratorial lowering of his voice. "And Mr. Rathbone, our manager, is not present, nor are the storage accountants, nor the clerks—only me, Pedro—shall we say one dollar per year?"

"Fifty dollars!" I exclaimed, having given no thought at all to the fact that if we did locate the trunk (which, frankly, I seriously doubted), we would have to pay the accumulation of storage fees.

On the other hand I had only seven dollars in my pocket and the checkbook of an overdrawn bank account.

"We'll give you fifty dollars and an extra ten dollars if you get us the trunk in a hurry," Hortense said, pulling a wad of bills from her purse and holding them up in front of the watchman's face.

"You see," she added coyly, "my great-grandmother's wedding dress is inside, and we're about to get married, and the dress has to be taken to a dressmaker who is entering the hospital next week for a kidney transplant, and she's the only one who knows anything about that old-fashioned kind of Spanish lace and embroidery—"

Well, as Mona Pariss would say, to make a long story short, less than two hours later we were lugging or rather dragging the trunk—an enormous old-fashioned brass-studded trunk with faded stickers of hotels and ocean liners still visible under the water-clogged layers of dust—to the elevator of my apartment building, and finally there it was on display in the very center of the living room rug, an almost terrifying relic or grave robbers' trophy, and neither of us rushed to traffic with the locks and latches, but continued to slump on the couch, staring at it as if inadvertently we had committed a sacrilege.

13

And like an unidentifiable unexplainable archeological find Mona Pariss' trunk remained there in the center of the living room where Hortense and I had dragged it, unopened, slightly sinister and forbidding.

And it remained there all that night. For Hortense had to leave on a late flight to Atlanta where she was to discuss and arrange with her rich uncle the details and technicalities of what by now had become *our* trip to Africa.

Just before dawn, however, having fallen asleep listening to one of those marathon radio talk shows—this one on the subject of UFO's and the so-called Bermuda Triangle (where apparently a number of planes and ships have been swallowed up into the sea or swept up into outer space, one of the great mysteries of all history according to the expert whose droning voice was penetrating my uneasy sleep) I woke up with a start, remembering that I had a hammer and chisel buried among other useless utensils in the bottom shelf of the cupboard in the kitchen.

Suddenly wide awake, the night sky outside the window brightening into an eerie glow, I turned on every light in the apartment, fumbled through the cast-off objects on the bottom shelf, and finally found the hammer and chisel and nervously rushed to the trunk, determined to break it open.

At first delicately, concerned that I might awaken the neighbors who might then call the police, I began to chisel the ancient brass lock.

But then impatience, or perhaps terror, took possession of me and my blows became louder, almost savagely frantic, until with one final crushing blow the lock was torn from the brass studs that held it and the curved coffin-like lid of Mona Pariss' trunk sprang open in a cloud of musty dust, so fine and powdery that instinctively I clenched shut my eyes as I was taught to do in the army in case of a tear gas attack.

The first thing I saw when the powdery dust cleared away was a yellowing newspaper with headlines announcing the election of Calvin Coolidge, the old newspaper serving evidently as a protective covering for the contents of the trunk. For a moment I was distracted by the advertisements on the inside pages of the old *Herald Tribune*, especially the price for a double-breasted man's suit $24.50 with two pairs of trousers. But quickly I tossed the crumbling newspaper aside and uncovered a layer of neatly folded theatrical costumes, most with beaded decorations and fringes. Pushing these aside, there was another layer of outfits, these of faded white silk, long angel-like costumes. There was a Princess Eugenie hat, some silk petticoats, silk stockings, two corsets, a carelessly bunched bundle of brand new men's ties, mostly conservative gray or dark blue polka dots, two Frenchy maid uniforms, complete with tiny aprons, and several all-black working uniforms. Strangely there was only one pair of shoes, a green silk covered pair of high heels which had the look of never having been worn. Then there was another layer of newspapers. These were newspapers of the Negro community, *The Pittsburgh Courier*, the *Amsterdam News*, and a tabloid-type newspaper from Orlando County, crudely printed and mainly containing church advertisements and birth and death notices, called *The Colored Orlando Voice*.

I was about to cast this newspaper aside to get at the remainder of the contents of the trunk when a news item on the bottom of the front page caught my attention. "DEATH OF FATHER OF LOCAL STAR MONA PARISS LOSS TO COLORED COMMUNITY." The date of the newspaper was Monday, April 9, 1927. . . .

I was by then too eager to get to the bottom of the trunk to pause to read the brief account that formed the body of the news item, but I carefully laid it aside, certain that the news story would cast some light on that part of Mona Pariss' story that I had so far neglected, her later relationship with the community where she had been raised, and, especially, her later relationship with her father.

But as soon as I removed this newspaper from the trunk I discovered that beneath it there was nothing of noteworthy importance except a few menus from European restaurants—artfully decorated souvenirs for the tourist trade, a visiting card bearing a crest and the name David Drives, Esq., with no handwriting on it, and a tangled mess of faded and tarnished silk scarves bundled up like dirty laundry.

But beneath all this was a small yellowish Kodak snapshot of a handsome young man in a Pullman porter's uniform who I could only assume was none other than Doc.

Something about the photograph, the fact that it was wrinkled and showed evidence of much handling, perhaps even moist kisses, reminded me of certain cheaply-painted portraits of saints that one often finds in the possession of peasants in Catholic countries.

Doc was dressed all in white and sported a carefully trimmed goatee. And though wearing his Pullman porter's uniform, he was wearing one of those wide-brimmed white hats of the period, at a cocky angle, and on his feet beneath the meticulously pressed Pullman porter trousers, they too white—though it had always been my impression that such trousers would have been navy blue or black—was a pair of apparently very expensive alligator skin shoes.

The photograph must have been taken during one of the layovers of whatever train he was working on at the time, for he was standing all alone at the top of the steps leading to what looked like the dining or parlour car, a suave smile on his face, his arm extending in a condescending wave to some imaginary welcoming committee—the wave of an arriving ambassador.

I took the photograph and placed it on my cocktail table and poured myself a drink and sat there until long after dawn staring at it as one would stare at some rare work of art struggling to unravel the mystery created by the artist.

And I remained sitting there until it was time for *The Today Show*, at which time I forced myself out of the chair I was seated on, piled all the dusty and mysterious shrouded mementos of Mona Pariss' past back into the trunk, taking only the crumbling copy of the *Orlando Colored Voice* to place beside the photograph for further examination—and then I shut the lid of the trunk and dragged it out to the cleansing morning sunlight sweeping my terrace from the direction of Kennedy Airport.

I had just settled down to hear what Barbara Walters was saying about the morning's guests when the phone rang, and, certain that it was a call from Hortense informing me of her safe arrival in Atlanta, I rushed to answer. Instead it was a tearful phone call from Gracie who announced, without even tactfully asking me whether I was alone, that she had to talk to me and that she would be over in a cab within the next hour.

14

Actually almost three hours passed before she arrived, and, since it was a Sunday, nearly lunchtime, I suggested that we take a walk in Central Park and then have a late lunch at the Tavern on the Green.

Though her voice had been tearful and distraught on the phone, now she was calm and poised, not her workday executive supercharged self, but a somewhat subdued Sunday-quiet Gracie.

She even refused a drink, admitting that she had taken a number of valium capsules the night before. But nevertheless I could sense a kind of tense urgency in her manner, mainly revealed by an unconscious clenching of her fingers and an impatient tapping of her feet, that placed me on guard that something unusual was on her mind.

We walked through the strolling couples, dodged the dogged bicyclists, and finally found a secluded spot near the lake beneath a flowering tree where we stretched out to take advantage of the brief appearance of the sun from behind a herd of puffy clouds headed out to sea.

So nearly twenty minutes went by while we just gazed up at the sky through the filtered sunlight of the trees with squirrels scampering about boldly and the shouts of a Puerto Rican baseball game punctuating the silence of our concentrated inner thoughts.

Then, calmly and quietly at first, almost philosophically, and then with accelerating rage, Gracie began to talk.

"All my life practically, my mother worked as a maid. Even after I got married and was pretty well off—Bob was working in an advertising agency as a vice-president at the time—she insisted on taking all my underwear and Bob's shirts and wash and iron them herself, even though we were paying her rent and giving her something like two hundred a month spending money. But most of her life, she worked as a maid, and that was the way she was conditioned to look at life, serving those better off, taking orders no matter in what kind of refined voice they were given, thankful for Thursdays and Sundays off. Christ, you've seen them on the Fifth Avenue buses around nine o'clock in the morning, their feet hurting, their crummy uniforms, their cast-off clothing, their sad resigned expressions—

"That wasn't for me, I was not getting myself into that bag, not even the secretarial bag which is what white girls pretend they are, anything except maids. I even thought of becoming an airline hostess, but what's that if not a maid—and besides I didn't have the *Playboy* figure, and I'm nobody's easy smiler.

"Well, you know how things changed after the riots? Everybody scrambling over themselves looking for a token nigger? Well, I applied and was accepted at Vassar. What the hell. If niggers was the new name of the game in colleges, why not try for the best?

"So I ended up the river with a white roommate, a dyke. But she meant well, and she didn't bother me, and she could really write. Christ, we would discuss books all night sometimes. We got to be good friends and she got me this job on the campus magazine, a literary magazine. And that's how I got my first editing experience. Everything I knew about editing and writing, I learned from her. Then, the end of her junior year, she started popping pills and killed herself. Rich, smart, talented, good family, automobiles you know—not selling, manufacturing them. I can't say I was particularly broken up. What white people do is their own business; I mean, if being a dyke, popping pills, and killing yourself is their bag, why not? So I became editor of the literary magazine and got a new roommate, a rich nigger bitch from Atlanta, Hortense Schiller's older sister.

"By now there were enough niggers on campus so that you could feel almost like you were big house niggers living on a fancy plantation. Augusta—that was Hortense's sister's name—and me got the idea of starting a magazine directed to a mass audience of Black women, women like my mother. Maids, short-order cooks, garment industry workers. In those days we were gung-ho in radical feminist politics like all the rich bitches. We had an idea we could push on the Black Revolution with a magazine like that.

"Well anyway—if all this is boring you, just say so. I've been running like a scared jackrabbit for so long since I got my divorce from Bob, that I just haven't taken the time to figure out what the hell is going on with my life. . . .

"You met Bob, cool, front nigger in an ad agency, smart as a Jew boy with money, fierce as a Panther, but with a toothy smile and a locker room buddy-buddy come-on. He's the one brought me down to earth about the magazine. He had his agency marketing service run a computerized analysis of the market for that kind of publication. Women's Lib was taking over the nigger thing after Malcolm X was assassinated, and the corporations were falling all over themselves trying to herd the seething Black sub-proletariat into the middle class where they could buy all the goodies that kept the economy going. He said the magazine would work, but it had to have an angle that could compete with *Ebony*.

"Actually *New Black Woman Magazine* was his brainchild. We were screwing one night and he suddenly stops at the wrong moment and yells, 'New Black Woman!' "

"I thought he was calling me a name and wanted me to turn over and do a porno-flick for him. But since he was a genius copywriter—really a genius—he did that Dr. Feelgood commercial you used to hear on the Black stations long before somebody stole the name for a song. Anyway, with all his connections—he was big with the Ford Foundation niggers, and had a tremendous in with Henry Ford and the Urban Coalition, and the elections were coming up, and it didn't take too many buddy-buddy men's room conversations for him to convince some of his connections to phone the banks, and the first thing you know we were in business with financing and advertising commitments for at least a year.

"That was, let me see, exactly four and a half years ago just before the magazine business began to fall apart. You being a novelist and a college professor probably think that magazines just grow like topsy, but it's a dirty complicated business and a Black magazine, especially with a name like *New Black Woman Magazine*, the dirt is cleaner but it's still dirt and competition envy and niggerish backbiting and backmouthing is even worse than with a magazine like, say, *New York Magazine*. . . .

"But we worked. We fought, we were true believers and we put together a magazine that graphically, professionally, with first-rate writing wasn't second to any magazine on the stands. Just the other day I got the figures on our circulation and you know where the highest circulation is? The area just east and west of Chicago and south to Kansas City which means that a lot of white folks were reading our magazine. You know about our divorce. Bob had this thing about white women, and the weird thing is I introduced most of them to him, former classmates of mine at Vassar.

"But as a husband he wasn't worth shit. He was after something. If he hadn't made it on Madison Avenue after coming out of Harvard Business School he probably would have become a pusher or a pimp. After a while—and it had nothing to do with the whitefolks feminist movement, that's their bag—we couldn't even talk without being at each other's throats. So divorce, clean and easy and no hard feelings. And I built up the magazine, hired some fresh new talent including that bitch you're running off to Africa with—"

"And who you fired—"

"She wasn't good for the magazine, she's romantic and still thinks that Black Revolution is the French Revolution in Technicolor. She wasn't good for the magazine so I fired her. Period.

"But I didn't call up to talk about her. You say you're in love with her, I say you're going through a stage of premature male menopause.

"What I called you up to tell you was that late Friday afternoon we heard the rumor that our financial backing was being cut off, just like that.

"Yesterday I went to the office with Dr. Chang, our business manager, and we made some phone calls around to the various country clubs in Westchester and found out that it was true. No more money for *New Black Woman Magazine*, no explanation, money's tight everywhere, advertisers are not spending any money on magazines, only TV, the whole rational bit.

"But what's behind it is we're a nigger magazine and this isn't the year for niggers with our kind of independent approach. So no more herding the Black sub-proletariat into the middle classes in a hurry, they're putting up housing projects out in the desert with electrified fences around them if you ask me. Anyway, we can make about six more payrolls and run your series on Mona Pariss and then that's it, the end. I feel like shit, and I feel like crying on somebody's shoulder, and I feel like a stupid little girl and I wish you were my daddy and I need a man, spelled M-A-N, if you know what I'm talking about. So for Christ's sake, let's get something to eat—but not that Tavern on the Green on a Sunday with all those bicycle freaks and their health-spa tans, let's go up to Harlem and eat some greasy food, and listen to some funky music and get stinking nigger drunk. . . .

"But one more thing before we go uptown, don't go to Africa with that girl. She's no good for you, you deserve better, you might even consider shacking up with me, I've learned a lot about what it means to be a woman living with a man, I mean I have the feeling that you and me could make it. Besides going to Africa with that bitch is going to distract you from the Mona Pariss story, and even if we can't run the whole thing I'm sure with Bob's connections we can package it as a book and maybe even sell it to the movies. We could do it, believe me, I've got hunches about what can sell and what can't sell. Christ, I've asked you to marry me. That's sick, real sick. Come on, get off your ass and let's take the bus uptown."

15

There were strikes, storms, flooded highways and a statistically high number of automobile accidents on the highway to Kennedy Airport. My apartment was flooded through the night because of a tile blown off during the beginning of the post-midnight rainstorm, my bowels had been churning for three hours, I was reprimanded by the Department head for not turning in my attendance reports on time (actually the computer center was to blame), and I had been assaulted by a nursing student who thought she deserved an A instead of the C I gave her, though the paper she had turned in was an exact duplicate of a paper I still kept piled under my desk of three years before. Finally now Hortense and I were seated in the cab, our skimpy luggage piled in the front seat, finally on our way to Mother Africa—taking a trip, getting out of New York, running off together, but with the excuse of a "mission"—creating some kind of "liaison," private and unattached to any government agency, between Black businessmen (no one would dare identify themselves as Black Capitalists) and the African Liberation Movements for the purpose of financial rather than the usual rhetorical support.

Hortense made the whole scheme seem so logical and viable ("Did you hear anything about 'More Parks sausages, Maw—Please—' during the African famine?") that, even though I was suffering from a severe case of diarrhea contracted at the greasy restaurant Gracie and I had eaten in the day before, I found her enthusiasm and excitement totally infectious. And it was in the spirit of two young lovers eloping in the wake of a mad onslaught of passion that we checked in and boarded the Ghana Airlines plane and settled back in our seats with our pre-dinner drinks, the faded glitter of the Manhattan nightscape soon obliterated by a vastly spacious moonlit sky.

We had had our drinks, eaten the usual continental airline dinner, and fallen asleep, Hortense's head softly resting on my shoulder, when I suddenly awakened with a start: I had neglected to tell Miss Pariss that I was leaving for Africa and that I would be gone two weeks—in fact, I had an appointment with her that very night.

The vision of her waiting impatiently for me to knock at her door filled me with paralyzing remorse and an acute sense of guilt, and I became so agitated with diarrhea I had to wake up Hortense almost brutally and practically run down the aisle to the toilet, alarming the charming Black hostesses who probably were thinking, judging by the terrified look in their wide slanted eyes, that either I was some kind of nut or that I intended to hijack the plane.

Fortunately one of the toilets was available and with excruciating pain followed by almost blissful relief I explosively relieved myself and bathed my aching irritated bowels with the only balm available, Velvet After Shave Lotion.

When I returned to my seat, intimidated by the suspicious stares of the now-awakened passengers, students or diplomats and wives all wearing brand new New York suits or dresses, Hortense ordered two more drinks, claiming that she was unable to sleep and was afraid to take another sleeping pill along with the alcohol, and suddenly became very talkative, but talkative in an obsessive almost manic fashion that revealed a side to her character that I, in the eclipse-like blindness of love-at-first-sight, had never observed before:

"I don't believe it—you know, actually *going* to Africa. Why are you squirming around in your seat so much? Until we were actually taking off, I never thought we would actually be on our way to Africa. And flying in a Boeing 707, not packed like sardines in the hold of a slave ship. I can't believe we're actually going. When I asked my Uncle Teddy for the money, when I first got the idea, he asked me why the hell did I want to go to Africa when I could go on a tour of Europe. You know, I had to remind him that I had been to Europe twice when I was at Vassar—once on an art safari to Florence, Italy, and one summer bumming around the youth hostels with a couple of friends, white friends, of course.

"But neither trip was any big deal. It was like going to one famous restaurant you've read about in the papers or seen in some corny 1940 late movie, only with everything you hate about America, superior smiles on dumb blue-eyed faces, and a lot of graveyard antiques that you can see better at the Metropolitan Museum.

"But Africa. Where we come from. Our home! I'm so excited I could piss in my pants. . . ."

I nodded sleepily, on the verge of drifting off to a lurking nightmare, as her voice ran on and on unceasingly, like one of those learning records you play beneath your pillow while you sleep.

"'Forget Africa,' my uncle said. 'The sooner Black people forget Africa and realize they're right here in the bad old U.S.A. and start pushing their way to the feeding trough like the rest of the pigs, the better off the race will be . . .'

"He's the filthy rich one—but he's not stupid, and—Oh, I forgot, a life insurance company with a burial clause fringe benefit—

"What was I saying? He's never been to college but he knows how to make money, and he smells a good deal when he smells one. He voted for Nixon and believes in Black Capitalism, he believes in Capitalism period . . .

"All he knows is money, and next to money he loves his little baby Hortense. He doesn't have any kids of his own, officially—though he spends a lot of weekends in the backwoods in his Lincoln Continental loaded with expensive presents, so I imagine he has families scattered all over Georgia. You know—sex and the money drive, the big American hang-up—

"Well, he's got the big American hang-up and he wants Black people to get off their complaining asses and get some of the loot before the country goes under which he is convinced is going to happen like just before Noah's Ark. He's very religious—"

The plane suddenly sunk in an air pocket and the *fasten your seat belts please* sign flashed on, but Hortense continued to talk, completely unaffected by the undercurrent of fear that passed like a cold draft down the aisle, chilling every passenger and awakening babies and prodding the handsome Black stewardesses to a British stance of sangfroid.

As I fastened Hortense's seat belt, she having completely ignored the metallic voice from the loudspeaker, I turned and gazed at her face, realizing, perhaps for the first time since I fell in love with her, how young and fresh she was, a beautiful creature of not only a different younger generation than I, but of some as yet unformed genetic flowering. And again I felt the deadening weight of being shabby and professorial.

"There's one thing I don't understand," she continued as I longed to drift off into sleep, "why no one ever thought of this before—Black businessmen buying medicines and guns for the African Liberation Movements. I mean, sure we've got our Black Unity thing here in America, but it's mostly jive meetings and speeches. Here at least there's a chance to *do* something. All this Mother Africa shit—you know a couple of girl friends, Black girls I used to share an apartment with, all decided to spend the summer in Africa instead of going to Europe. So they bought all these robes from the Ashanti Shop, and corn-rowed their hair and shaped up their Afros, and you know what they said when they got back—they couldn't stand the food, and the Africans stared at them like they were freaks and were always trying to rip them off.

"I mean, they expected there would be a delegation of chiefs decked out in gold with warriors performing spear dances to welcome them 'home.' Sometimes—well, I hate to say it, but sometimes I think Black Americans are more American than the white ethnic Americans, only they've got this slavery thing to give them some kind of special pedigree—"

Those were the last words I remember, because after falling

into a deep sleep, the next thing I remember was that the fasten-your-seat-belt sign was on again and we were circling over the airport in Accra.

Hortense, as usual, was so excited that she ignored the sign and was standing up fumbling for her luggage in the rack over our seats until a tall beautiful hostess sternly admonished her to "please observe the regulations."

It was while we were finishing our emigration formalities that I must have fainted. For the last thing I remember was a young smiling Black face with a military cap leaning over me asking in an amused yet officious deep voice:

"Has the gentleman been overly imbibing while inflight from the United States?"

The next thing I knew I was in bed in a blindingly white hospital room (not a private room as I shall explain later) with three Black doctors, two nurses—one African, the other Chinese—gathered around my bed, all armed with the usual polished instruments of the medical profession, and the usual serious concerned, yet slightly blasé, expression of medical practitioners all over the world.

The strange thing, in recollection, is that I didn't recognize Hortense when she edged her way through the doctors and nurses and leaned over the spotless linen to give me a comforting kiss.

"Who is she?" I thought. "One of my students perhaps?"

By then the doctors and nurses had discreetly moved en masse to the far end of the ward, one doctor and the Chinese nurse pausing to examine a patient in the bed next to the lobby door.

"Don't worry, darling," Hortense said, pulling up a chair and caressing my sweating forehead with a brand new white linen handkerchief she must have just bought for the purpose, since I had never seen her with a handkerchief before. Indeed, it was the handkerchief that fulminated me with a sense of foreboding and alarm.

"What happened?"

"Don't worry, darling—the doctors assured me you'll be up and well in a little more than a week—"

"But what happened? What am I doing in this hospital?"

"What happened," she said in a matter-of-fact tone of voice, "was that you fainted just after we went through emigration. Just like that, you just kind of crumpled up like a rag doll and fell on the floor. I was scared as hell. I thought you had had a heart attack or were subject to epileptic fits and hadn't told me. After all, we've only known each other a little over a month, that is, really known each other, if you know what I mean.

"But don't you worry, darling. The doctors are fantastic. One of them interned in Edinburgh, and the other got his training in Russia, and they brought in a young doctor who just finished his internship at Harlem Hospital. The doctor who was trained in Russia thinks you are suffering from a psychosomatic trauma brought on by excessive drinking and the pressurized cabin of the plane. The one trained in Scotland thinks you have malaria complicated by a serious attack of food poisoning and dysentery. The Harlem-trained doctor wants to withhold diagnosis until further observation. So you'll be staying here in the hospital for a week or so—"

"But what about our mission—our liaison with the Liberation Movements?"

"Oh, that's all taken care of," she said breezily. "I have all the contacts and letters of introduction and, in a way, they don't really know anything about you—you know how tense and suspicious revolutionaries have to be, they might have thought you were some kind of CIA agent or something—"

"That's a terrible thing to say, you know me better than that—ohh, call a nurse, I have to run to the bathroom—"

"Orders are that you are to stay in bed. There's a bed pan in that cabinet next to the electric fan. Here, I'll get it for you—"

I had no choice but to relieve myself in a noisy splattering mess while Hortense just sat there in her tight-fitting jeans, smiling and looking on with clinical fascination.

"I've never seen a man do that before—no kidding, this is the first time, really the absolutely first time I've seen a man do it like that in that position—"

"Hortense, you're a monster—I don't feel like joking, I feel terrible, I feel as if I'm going to die, and my ass itches something terrible—"

"Call the nurse, damn it, ring that goddamned buzzer—"

The nurse came, the part-Chinese nurse, and asked politely if there was something she could do.

"His ass is itching—" Hortense said calmly, but with a mischievous glint in her eyes.

"Ass is itching—I do not understand—"

"I have just had a convulsive bowel movement and my intestinal canal burns like someone stuck a firecracker up it and set it off—"

The Chinese nurse politely placed her hand over her mouth to suppress a giggle, and she bathed me gently.

"Wait—I come back in just a moment—" she said when she finished.

While she was away I attacked Hortense in angrier tones than I had ever spoken to her with.

"This is no joke—I'm sicker than a dog, and I'm stuck in this godforsaken hospital in the heart of Africa, and you sit there and find it funny that I'm on the point of death. This isn't like you, Hortense. I expected more compassion from you—after all we've been through together—"

"But darling, don't take everything so seriously—"

"You mean my death means nothing to you—?"

"You're not going to die, you only have a mild case of food poisoning or something. Why do you always have to be so dramatic about everything? Does it have something to do with the fact that you're a creative person, a novelist—?"

"I'm not worried about myself," I said in a calmer voice, struggling to recover some kind of mature self-control.

The Chinese nurse returned so silently that she was standing over me with a syringe before I realized that she had returned.

"Please turn over and lower the bottom of your pajamas," she said.

I glanced suspiciously, more than a little alarmed, almost appealingly, at Hortense—who was suppressing a giggle.

"Show the pretty nurse what a nice ass you have," she whispered, leaning over and again wiping my forehead with that macabre white linen handkerchief that kept forcing me to think of Mary wiping the forehead of the suffering Christ on the Cross.

"Lower, please," the nurse said.

And in an instant she had injected some wine-colored liquid into my buttocks from a vial.

"That should relieve your discomfort," she said, "and also help you get some sleep—"

"Sleep! I can't sleep now—we've got to catch that Pan Am flight to Zambia in a few—"

Whatever the nurse injected into my buttocks worked fast. I was floating on clouds, blissfully, as Hortense kissed me lovingly on the lips, and tickled her tongue sexily against my teeth.

"Don't worry about the mission, my darling. Everything has been arranged. The representative from the Central Committee was at the airport. I couldn't introduce you to him because you had just fainted. So don't worry. I will be in very good hands. I am to be escorted personally to headquarters. So bye, bye, darling. I'll write every single day and if it's at all possible I'll phone you—Now have a nice peaceful sleep—"

16

That must have been the longest and sweetest sleep in my life, for I awoke smiling and I felt like a newborn babe. It was morning, just after dawn; the shutters were not closed and the light in the ward was a muted garden party light filtered softly through the curtains.

Still smiling like a drugged idiot, I had just turned over toward the wall, curled up into a fetus position in an attempt to drift back to sleep when a soft Harlem-inflected voice completely disoriented me as to where I was in the world:

"Hey, man, how you feelin'? What you puttin' down? All rolled up in a ball like a wino tryin' ta get some sleep on the back row of the A train?"

It was the young African doctor who had received his medical training at the Columbia School of Medicine and Harlem Hospital.

"Good morning, doctor," I said, still on the prenatal high trip. "I feel fine—never felt better in my life—"

A nurse passed with a breakfast tray, and while she was placing it on the rolling cart near my bed, he quickly reverted to his official professional manner, though he gave me a wink and slyly patted the pert nurse on the ass.

"I've been studying your charts and talking with the other doctors. We've finally agreed that you have abdominal and intestinal complications due to some kind of food poisoning. But since the young lady who arrived with you said you haven't eaten any native cooking here in Accra, and airline food is the same the world over, sanitized and rendered completely tasteless by infrared cooking, the only possibility is that you must have eaten something that is responsible for your condition while you were in the U.S. Is that possible, do you think?"

"I am afraid it's not only possible, that's exactly what happened—then what I have is not serious?"

"Well, there is another complication which we are watching carefully, at least that is my job—and it is for that reason that you must remain here under observation for at least a week. Tests show the possibility of viral hepatitis—"

"You mean I have to stay here a whole week while you doctors make up your minds what is wrong with me?"

"I have not been practicing long, but let me tell you something, man—if I learned one thing in Harlem Hospital, man, you better believe it—medicine is nobody's exact science. So why don't you just relax and enjoy your stay in this brand new hospital, one of the finest in all Africa—and with the finest chicks, if you dig what I mean?"

"But I've come all this distance to see Africa—"

"How long you been living in New York?"

"Eight years or so on and off—"

"Well, you already seen Africa! Man, you got more lions and tigers in the Bronx Zoo than you'll ever see over here. As for witch doctors, just take a walk down East End Avenue on the East Side and count the number of psychiatrists' offices—Man, I counted twenty-seven in *one* town house one Sunday I was taking a walk to see how the better half live. So, brother, just you lay back there and enjoy yourself, consider this a vacation, and if the food isn't to your liking, just ask for Dr. Kufu. And keep your hands off that Chinese chick, she don't play . . ."

At the far end of the ward, a team of nurses was placing a wheeled curtain around one of the beds. Dr. Kufu, a short fat mustached man in his late twenties and with rhythmic movements to his abnormally long arms, rushed in that direction, though not before whispering in my ear:

"Dig you later . . ."

So there was nothing to do but settle down and flow with the hospital routine—tests, breakfast, blood samples, lunch, a walk around the ward, more tests, more blood samples, and blissful sleep. I was suspended in a dream of whiteness and medical instruments, half-drugged most of the time, constantly smiling at everything and everyone, back in mother's womb—the womb of Mother Africa, of course—nothing to do, nothing to say, nothing to think. And so, eight uneventful days went by, and still no word—no letter, no telephone call, no telegram—from Hortense. Until the morning of the ninth day in the hospital.

The envelope that rested next to the toast on my breakfast tray was long, the paper rather coarse and heavy of a type I have seen on letters from Central Europe, the stamp (or stamps, for there were many, all of scenic views or jungle animals) enormous, and bore many officious rubber stamps.

From the Vassar side-slanted scroll I knew immediately that it was from Hortense, and whether from the fat oversized envelope, the exotic enormous stamps, or the officious rubber stamps, I was both reluctant and impatient to rip it open—instead, I forced myself to chew each mouthful of breakfast food at least ten times, wait until my heartbeat had become normal (after eight days in the hospital I had begun to think in medical terms and was maniacally and acutely aware of even the most minor bodily functioning), and after the tray had been removed and I knew that there would be a half-hour interval before Dr. Kufu's morning rounds, I painstakingly opened it, even taking care that I did not disturb the perforations of the stamps which had almost overlapped one end of the letter.

"Darling, my darling," the letter began. And before reading the rest of the contents I felt the sudden compulsion to leaf through the five thin rice-paper pages to the end and read the signature which read with ominous sincerity: "Yours for eternal friendship, Hortense Schiller. . . ."

So I fought down the insidious cancer growth of foreboding and forced my mood into one of loving optimism and started at the beginning of the letter as though I hadn't cheated and read the sign-off.

"Darling, my darling—my dearest dearest darling. You have no idea with what a feeling of awe and wonder I take my ballpoint pen in hand to write you at last and share with you some of the most fabulous experiences I have ever had in my life. Georges Mantu, the member of the Information Services of the Commandos who met me at the airport, has proven himself to be absolutely *precious.* He speaks English perfectly though he learned it in, of all places, Bulgaria, where he attended the University of Sophia or is it Sofia, anyway he speaks English with a really cute accent and is *very intelligent*, I mean really *hip*, a Catholic-Marxist-Revolutionary whatever that is, I mean I've never heard of that ideological position in the States. Have you? I mean Angela Davis is a Marcusian Marxist, but then she's a sister from my old hometown, Atlanta, and went to Brandeis U. But Georges has been a perfect doll in *every* way. He is in absolute sympathy with the offer of aid to their cause from Black Americans whether they be businessmen or not, especially as regards medicines and guns. He thinks that there should be a much greater participation on the part of our dispersed Black brothers and sisters in the Americas, as he calls it, with the African Liberation Movements, and I couldn't agree with him more. I mean, all this rhetorical bullshit and TV talk shows aren't molding our common destinies worth a shit. He has spoken with his superior *officers* (he is a Colonel himself, though he wears the uniform of a common soldier and enjoys no special privileges). No Shaft in Africa bullshit here! This is the *real thing*! As he puts it, revolution is like knitting a sweater, a stitch at a time until suddenly the whole sweater has arms and a neck and is a beautiful thing to behold, a work of infinite patience and love. And speaking of love, Georges and I have fallen in love with each other, suddenly, just like that. Destiny brought us together and you were the agent of that destiny and I shall be eternally grateful to you for all you have done for me and taught me. We are perfect for each other, Georges and I, I mean. Yesterday we were married in a tiny little chapel (Catholic) in the bush by a Black Revolutionary priest, that's right—he works for the Revolution and sometimes even goes out on patrols at night, *carrying a gun*! After the ceremony, which was very simple and fast, there was a little party around a campfire, and we drank beer and I taught some of the soldiers the latest Harlem dances. It was all very moving. No music, except for five minutes on the camp receiver, James Brown, I believe, though I was in such a trance about it all I hardly remember, and no drums. These commandos don't use drums at all. Would you believe it? No drums. And they're a little puritanical, if you know what I mean, so I have to watch my language and act like a lady, and it's a damn good thing I went to Vassar, I mean, these men mean business and when they laugh or smile it's even scarier than when their faces are serious. So now I am Mrs. Georges Mantu, so I guess that's the end of Hortense Schiller—I never liked Schiller as a poet anyway, he was too, well, you know, being a novelist and a poet and a professor yourself, so German romantic nationalistic, all that culture trip. And to think I used to be proud my last name was Schiller! Well, that's life, isn't it? I love you for all you have done for me, and taught me. Georges' superior officers in the Central Council have given him a three-month leave to make a speaking tour before Black businessmen audiences in the U.S. for the purpose of stirring up interest in their cause, and of course I will be handling most of the P.A. work for that. So have a pleasant trip back. I heard through the grapevine that you're doing fine and should be ready to be released from the hospital by the time this reaches you, so 'Yours for Eternal Friendship' Hortense Schiller. . . ."

17

New York that August seemed to me to be a combination of a Latin carnival and open house day in the archeological remains of a cemetery, overcrowded with natives dressed like tourists and tourists with the numbed expressionless look of natives.

Struggling with my bags, I entered my apartment building and the new Protective Agency guard, a jet black Haitian with oiled straightened hair, asked me if I were a resident, even though I opened the door of the entrance hall with my own key.

The only change in my tiny apartment on the top floor with its marvelous view of Manhattan (an oasis, the only unchangeable point of reference in my disaster-ridden existence) was the stink coming from the refrigerator, a combination of rotting eggs and spoiled meat. Hortense had defrosted the refrigerator but had neglected to remove the food contents. Hortense, that beautiful young bitch, how could she do this to me? Self-pity, loneliness, and the fact that my telephone had been turned off for non-payment of my last bill triggered a nauseous chemical reaction in my psyche and I resolved to become a self-defeated recluse. Immediately, I began to drink myself into a stupor and began talking to myself. I played "our" Stevie Wonder record over and over again and danced with myself. I refused to eat anything but candied yams and peanuts. I refused to unpack my bag. Alternately I undressed and dressed, following some time-gap pattern established while I was in the hospital in Accra. I slept when the scotch paralyzed me and in that manner day and night merged into a foggy formless dimension punctuated only by my mad ravings or vomiting or nightmares which were more like old movies I had walked through before. My only pleasure, if one may call it such, consisted of making occasional trips to the bathroom mirror to watch myself age, hour by hour, minute by minute, second by second, micro-second by micro-second.

I was like a child making a last-minute change in identity before a Hallowe'en party. I looked awful, and contrived to further my monster appearance by contorting my face into strange lizard-like masks.

No. I was *enjoying* myself: I was wallowing in the filth of a vanished self-esteem, like a prophet wallows in the ecstasy of his own excrement in his search for God.

Even sadness was not written into the script of my solitary orgy of madness. Exaltation. Yes. But not sadness. How could I be sad by the betrayal of a love that was itself a betrayal of my own self-love? In retrospect, the dominant emotions were (1) humiliation (2) frustration at the loss of a favorite toy (3) the terrifying realization that there is no such thing as adulthood or manhood or growing up, that one is born a child and remains a child until the end. Only the physical masks change, and it was that change of physical masks—horror masks of aging—that most fascinated me in the five days I remained locked up in my apartment.

Two events, unrelated, brought me to my senses, or at least relatively so. The first was a knock at the door, very insistent, which at first I pretended to ignore but which, after a few minutes, I responded to (fortunately I was dressed in filthy pajamas, for in the state I was in, I well might have appeared to them naked). When I opened the door, three children from the Catholic Church around the corner asked me "mister" if I wanted to buy a chance on a color TV set. But before I could stammer a reply, they had already made a hasty and terrified retreat toward the elevator.

The second event occurred after I realized that I had finished the last bottle of scotch and, in a frantic search through the apartment for a bottle I had hidden somewhere a year before during a wild hectic party, behind the drain pipe on the terrace, if what was left of my muddled memory was correct, I stumbled and fell on my face over Mona Pariss' trunk, which had remained in the exact position where I had dragged it, now seemingly years before, just outside the sliding glass doors of the terrace.

18

Nearly myself (but which self after the monster changes of identity I had just experimented with?), bathed, after-shave-lotioned, superbly sharp, ultra cool in the very same Superfly, white, Italian-styled suit, white wide-brimmed hat, and white fancy collared nylon shirt I had bought for my trip to Africa (the safari suit still neatly folded in the bottom of my suitcase for the aborted journey with the commandos in the jungle camps), forced finally into a dizzy descent to urban reality by an alarming examination of the stack of bills to be paid that had accumulated during my absence, including a registered letter from a collection agency, I acquired sufficient sanity to resolve to finish up once and for all the series of articles on Mona Pariss with the hope of an advance, or at least a cash loan on an advance, from Gracie (who still didn't know that I had returned), to tide me over until my next paycheck from the college would arrive, a few days before the beginning of classes, less than three weeks away.

So, thus attired, I crossed Broadway with confident hipster authority, and turned down the side street toward Riverside

Drive, headed for the dilapidated town house where Mona Pariss and Reverend Grooms lived.

But the moment I saw the demolition equipment and the trucks blocking the street in front of the building, I knew immediately that I might have arrived too late. Nearly a third of the building had already been torn down. The entrance hall was still intact, but the side of the building nearest Riverside Drive was gutted as in those World War II photographs of bombed buildings in Germany.

Frantically, I entered the downstairs hallway, afraid that the demolition hammers would strike at any moment, and ran up the stairs to the landing.

The door to Reverend Grooms' apartment was off its hinges and wide open. There was dog excrement in the doorway and debris scattered all over the floor. All the furniture had been removed except for one overturned Pullman dining car table with a smashed leg.

The debris and filth, the desolation of the empty apartment that contrasted so vividly with the deluxe Pullman car atmosphere of that night so long ago when he had invited Hortense and me to dinner, filled me with a blood-stopping sense of foreboding.

Turning away from the depressing view, I rushed across the landing to Miss Pariss' door and knocked so loud and hard that my fists were bruised. After what seemed to be almost half an hour, though an impatient glance at my watch showed that only three minutes had passed, I heard sounds of stirring inside, and, after a long silent pause, as though whoever inside was peering out through some invisible peep-hole, the door opened and I was face to face again with Miss Pariss, and it was almost as if I were seeing her for the first time.

She was wearing one of her Chinese embroidered robes, but it was so wrinkled and stained that she must have been wearing nothing else for weeks. Her face, as with most people who have aged to the limit of biological change, had become childlike, as had her expression, though obviously she was very ill and smelled as though she had been drinking Reverend Grooms' red Gallo wine instead of her preferred scotch. She seemed not in the least surprised to see me—indeed, I had the disturbing feeling that she had been expecting me.

"Come on in, Doc," she said in a strangely altered tone of voice, a tone of voice with a singsong Chinese cadence to it: "I been waiting and waiting and waiting, and here you finally show up after all these years. . . ."

Then she laughed, a silly girlish laugh, and she lowered her head modestly and fluttered her fossil-etched eyelids.

"You Pullman porters just like them there trains you all travel on—you might be late but you always arrive on time. . . ."

I followed her into her apartment which was in almost total darkness, all the shades drawn, the windows sealed, a candle enclosed in a cut-off beer bottle the only source of light.

"They turned off all my electricity, about a week after Reverend Grooms passed away. He got a fairly decent burial, though the funeral wasn't much, no relatives, no flowers. The welfare people paid, but not even his social worker showed up at the ceremony—Doc, where you been all this time?"

She turned and placed her hands on her wasted hips coyly and inclined her head to one side and began studying me, the hint of a smile on her colorless lips:

"Doc, no wonder they say you so devilish looking, all dressed in white like that. You even better looking than the last time I saw you. What you do with your goatee? Them Pullman supervisors make you shave it off? Tell you the honest truth—no offense meant—I think you better looking without your goatee than with it. I think it was the goatee made the preacher in the choir tell me you was the devil in disguise—"

I was still standing bewildered and awed by her obviously deranged behavior, when she turned from lighting another candle which she placed in the middle of the table and said:

"Have you a seat over there on the divan, youngblood—I'll get you a glass of red Gallo wine to refresh you after your trip. Reverend Grooms left nearly six gallons hidden in his closet. He must a bought them the same day he won the New York State lottery. I favors scotch myself but lately I been finishing up the Reverend's wine 'cause it would be sacrilegious to throw it away, that's what I figgers—him being all the folks I had left in the world, and when your last friend passes on, there ain't much left to hang your heart on now, is there? We fought and we made up and we carried on something terrible like we was enemies, like the time he wanted to make that gypsy costume in *River Boat Time* solid gold stead of red *and* gold, gypsies ain't no golden angels, and that time in Paris when he said I was foolin' around with the King's son, I ain't never fooled around with no man, he knew that, he should have known it, he was with me all those years of my life, traveling halfway round the world, designing my costumes and hairstyles, and escorting me when an escort was *rigueur*, but I ain't never loved no other man, ever since that night at the Gospel Festival down home when I was a little girl, and the moon shining on you like you was the angel of the Lord, and now you're back from your trip, and I don't mind saying you sure look more like an angel than ever without that goatee—though, I sure enjoyed looking at you with that goatee on, even though the preacher he say you is the devil in disguise. You sit there on that divan, Doc, while I fetch you some of Reverend Grooms' communion wine—hee! hee!—Lord, that wino bum would kill me if he heard me callin' his red Gallo wine communion wine—"

I solemnly accepted the filthy glass of red wine as though it were indeed a goblet of gold and slowly sipped the bitter vinegar-tasting liquid but said nothing, for there was nothing I could say or even think of saying, so under a spell of total enchantment was I, neither knowing nor caring upon which plane of time and memory and myth I had been bewitched into by the incantation of her words. She sat down beside me and for a very long time even the crashing and banging sounds of demolition outside on the street were absorbed into the sponge-like silence that surrounded her like an angelic neon glow in the cavernous darkness of the room, only dimly eerily lit as during the eclipse of the sun by the candle stump flames flickering in response to some barely perceptible draft.

"But your life, Miss Pariss—your life, such a contribution—" I heard myself saying.

"My life ain't been worth shit—all I did was sing what was in my heart and what the Good Lord He told me to sing—"

"But your life, the immense gift of your talent," I repeated; "it has been an inspiration the world should know about. You are an important chapter in the history of Black Americans—"

"Doc, what kind of jive talk you putting down on me?" she said, giggling. "I ain't nobody's history, Doc, cause I ain't dead—You talkin' to Mona Pariss, Doc—you ain't talkin' to no ghost—"

Silence, terrible, pregnant.

"Doc, you sure talk funny—Where you been on this trip? New Orleans?"

"It's been a long long trip, Miss Pariss—I'm glad I'm back—"

"I'm glad you back too—you want something to eat, Doc? You want me to fix you some—?"

Her head fell back against the divan, like a puppet's head when the strings are released, and she seemed to be thinking disturbing thoughts with her eyes closed, because her child-like brow was furrowed and her gray lips had a downward cast.

"History is what people *say* about you," she said after a while. "Not what you say about yourself. History is what people *say* you do, not what you do yourself . . ."

She was staring at me as though she were frightened by what she said, or by what she was about to say. Then, with a sudden thrust, she reached out and grabbed hold of my hand, and squeezed it almost painfully tight in her cold bony fingers.

"Are you healed, Doc? Did those conjure women heal you of your secret ailment?"

And there was yet another long silence, and memories old and recent marched by, and coagulated into presences, ghosts, motionless tableaus . . .

(*"Doc, he was something else—I mean, he was fast! As it happened that night, all us younger girls, we slept in a peanut warehouse which the Goober Peanut Company let the church committee use as a kind of dormitory, so long about midnight I hear this whistling outside the window, and I kind of know even though I'm floating off somewhere in a dream that it was Doc whistling out there under the moon, and anyway I couldn't sleep even though I was dreaming on account of being so young with all that hot blood churning me into buttermilk. So I gets off the cot and goes to the window, and there he is standing there in his white suit and Brilliantined goatee with the full moon shining down upon him just like he was the angel of the Lord, and when he motions for me to come out, well, I just slipped into my dress like I was a sleepwalker or a zombie and snuck out of that peanut warehouse like it was all a part of the dream. And the first thing you know, there we are loving it up in the bushes down by the river—I don't mean intercoursing, I'll tell you about that later, but just hugging and kissing and loving it up like in a nice clean movie. And that was the first time I'd been with a man, and as far as I was concerned that was all what being with a man meant, just lying there in the bulrushes hugging and kissing like Cleopatra and the Prophet Moses. . . .*

"Well, sir, toward morning, when those mists was coming over the river and turning all pink and golden with the rising of the sun, I turned over and saw Doc lying there like a sleeping prince and I woke him up and told him I wanted some more hugging and kissing, that I was now ready for the real nitty-gritty, if you know what I mean—

"When I said that I could tell he was thinking and meditating about what I said and staring at me like he was trying to figure me out, so I just kind of laid there resting and listening to the birds twittle, waiting until whatever he was thinking about would come manifest in his mind. So, finally he told me about how because of what happened to him in a train accident he never did it with girls, and that anyway a young girl like me would be better off staying a virgin all her life, dedicating herself to her art for the world and posterity, that way she would be like a priestess and have power

over men instead of men having power over her. Then after I lay there and let that sink in wondering why he was talking all crazy like that but believing every word of what he was saying because he being such a gentleman and a traveling man who knows the world, he finally turn to me and say: 'Little Angel, you got the sweetest singing voice this side of heaven and I'm going to take you with me and be your manager, because I'm tired of being a Pullman porter and we both special kind of people with a touch of the ghost world kings in our veins. Sweet little singing angel, you going to come away with me and leave this peanut plantation forever . . . .'")

Outside, an ambulance screamed by. And when it passed I heard her saying:

"Doc, I had this dream last night, that them Ku Klux Klanners they castrate you off like a pig but that it grow back on, that you was just telling me about the train accident so not to scare me, and that's how I knew you was coming back from the trip to New Orleans—"

"It wasn't New Orleans this time," I said, "it was a longer trip than that, a long long trip—"

"Well, folks with ghost king blood in their veins are naturally born traveling men, that's why I knew you would come back, that's why I been waitin' here for you all this time, waiting all my life for you to come back from your trip—and now, thank the Lord, here you is, all glowing and arraigned in white vestments like the angel of the Lord—"

"It *has* grown back," I said. "It was a miracle, but it *has* grown back—"

Was I going mad, were these words my words, my thoughts, was I completely under this obviously deranged and dying woman's spell? Again the strange journey through time and reality and myth. Where would it stop? Where was it all leading me to? Why had I been hoodooed into this obscurely fateful encounter?

"I got the unguents and the herb potions, Doc—Now you help yourself to some more of that red Gallo wine. . . ."

Then, again her head dangled back against the back of the divan, loosely, and she remained in a muscleless inclined position for such a long time that I thought she had fallen into a coma. But after five minutes or so, her eyes flickered open with an almost hallucinatory gleam, and she said, piercingly, almost prayerfully, at the same time as a sacred command:

"Doc, you come back just in time from your trip to New Orleans or wherever that train done took you—but now the miracle has taken place and it's grown back what the Ku Klux Klanners castrated off with their hunting knife, you got to do it tonight, you got to do it like you should've done it when we was in the bulrushes down by the river back home—"

"Do what?—I don't understand—"

"It grown back, ain't it? That's a sign from the Lord, it's a miracle that we got to respect, be a sacrilege if we disrespected the miracle of it growing back—We got to do it right, like the Lord created man and woman to begat and multiply and re-create the earth—"

She had taken off her Chinese embroidered stained robe and revealed her wasted yet child-like girlish body as in an ancient ritual of puberty, shyly, a profound solemn sense of the rituality of what she was doing. And she lay back on the divan, and in the dawn light or sunset glow (who could tell in the hourless glow of that dark flickering candlelit room), she placed a cushion back under her head, and in the innocence and frenzy of first love she touched my fingers tentatively and then seized them with the force of the passionate grasping to life that is both birth cry and death rattle and motioned for me to hurry, hurry, hurry. . . .

And I too took off my robes and became naked before her. And she saw that indeed the miracle had taken place, and her face glowed with a light of wonderment and immense joy and timid fear:

"Doc—Lord, the miracle has happened and you is a man again, a warrior man, a ghost king man. Doc, do it now. I don't got time, I can't wait to go fetch the unguents and the herb potions I had prepared so long, so long. . . ."

Her pubic hairs were the white snow caps of a child's model mountain, and I touched the edge of my erect penis to the almost invisible and wrinkled opening and felt the dampness of the morning or evening dew of the bulrushes, and the full moon shone down upon us and beyond the river as time flowed forever and ever and I gave a thrust and Mona Lisa let out a cry of pain and ecstasy and joy and then became suddenly heavy and while we were embraced she died in my arms. Her last words, barely audible, though well I remember them:

"You all together now, Doc, oh yes, Doc, you all together, those Ku Klux Klanners they castrated it off with they huntin' knife but it done grow back big, bigger than a tree, so do it now, Doc, do it right now, do it Doc, I ain't got much time. . . ."

ALSO BY

WILLIAM DEMBY

THE CATACOMBS

In this masterpiece of metafiction set in the Rome of the tumultuous 1960s, Black American expatriate Bill Demby narrates his attempts to write a novel about his friend Doris, a Black American actress working as one of Elizabeth Taylor's handmaidens in the film *Cleopatra*. Utterly dependent upon Doris for the development of his novel, Demby is both a participant in and observer of her life as she begins an affair with an Italian count. Demby's growing emotional and artistic involvement in the affair of his character-friend leads him on an existential quest for the meaning of truth and fiction, both lived and created, in a world torn by the social upheaval of the time period.

Fiction

KING COMUS

Past and present collide in William Demby's *King Comus*. In the present day, a Black American expat to Rome named D. reconnects with his former Army friend, Tillman, and their former commanding officer, Joe Stabat, to organize a gospel summit for the singer Little Antioch. In the 1940s, as D. becomes enmeshed in Tillman's large and boisterous family for the first time, Tillman recounts the story of his fabled ancestor King Comus. And in the early nineteenth century, master musician King Comus embarks on a grand journey to freedom from enslavement. In this time-bending tale of survival and kinship, the product of more than twenty years of literary labor, Demby weaves elements of the neo-slave narrative and Afrofuturism into a panoramic vision encompassing the forces of empire, race, gender, and religion.

Fiction

BEETLECREEK

After years of seclusion in the Black quarter of Beetlecreek, West Virginia, in the precarious 1930s, a retired carnival worker named Bill Trapp strikes up a chance friendship with Johnny Johnson, a Pittsburgh teenager transplanted into his uncle's home. Bill is white. Johnny is Black. Both are searching for acceptance, something that will give meaning to their lives. While Bill tries to court favor in the community, Johnny joins a local gang; meanwhile, their new friendship kindles hope that there is something for each of them beyond the bounds of Beetlecreek. But as the church society's Fall Festival approaches, the battle between the repressive small town and the aspirations of its trapped inhabitants comes to a nail-biting head. First published in 1950, *Beetlecreek* stands as a moving condemnation of provincialism and fundamentalism, and a classic of Black American literature. Both a critique of racial hypocrisy and a new direction for the African American novel, it occupies fresh territory that is neither the gritty realism of Richard Wright nor the ironic modernism of Ralph Ellison.

Fiction

VINTAGE BOOKS
Available wherever books are sold.
vintagebooks.com